# ONCE UPON A KISS GONE *Horribly* *Wrong*

Prequel to
'The Whickertons in Love' Series

BY BREE WOLF

WOLF PUBLISHING

**Once Upon a Kiss Gone Horribly Wrong by Bree Wolf**

Published by WOLF Publishing UG


Text by Bree Wolf
Cover Art by Victoria Cooper
Print ISBN: 978-3-98536-005-5
Ebook ISBN: 978-3-98536-004-8

WOLF Publishing - This is us:

*Two sisters, two personalities.. But only one big love!*

*Diving into a world of dreams..*

*...Romance, heartfelt emotions, lovable and witty characters, some humor, and some mystery! Because we want it all! Historical Romance at its best!*

Visit our website to learn all about us, our authors and books!

Sign up to our mailing list to receive first hand information on new releases, freebies and promotions as well as exclusive giveaways and sneak-peeks!

WWW.WOLF-PUBLISHING.COM

# Also by Bree Wolf

**The Whickertons in Love**

The WHICKERTONS IN LOVE is a new series by USA Today bestselling author BREE WOLF set in Regency-era England, portraying the at times turbulent ways the six Whickerton siblings search for love. If you enjoy wicked viscounts, brooding lords as well as head-strong ladies, fierce in their affections and daring in their search for their perfect match, then this new series is perfect for you!

#1 Once Upon a Devilishly Enchanting Kiss

#2 Once Upon a Temptingly Ruinous Kiss

#3 Once Upon an Irritatingly Magical Kiss

#4 Once Upon a Devastatingly Sweet Kiss

#5 Once Upon an Achingly Beautiful Kiss

#6 Once Upon an Accidentally Bewitching Kiss

*Prequel to the series:* Once Upon A Kiss Gone Horribly Wrong

# ONCE UPON A KISS GONE *Horribly Wrong*

# Prologue

*Somewhere in England, Winter 1790 (or a variation thereof)*
*Eleven years earlier*

The snow crunched under her feet as eight-year-old Annie Thatcher raced across the white meadow after her best friend, Tobias Hawke, second son to Viscount Barrington. Small flakes clung to her dark curls peeking out of her hood and settled on the tip of her nose, making her sneeze. Still, Annie pressed on even though her legs began to ache as she fought to keep up with Toby.

When he reached the edge of the frozen lake, he jumped in the air, a wide grin upon his red face. He roared in triumph and pulled his woolen hat off his head, throwing it in the air. "Yes, I made it. I told you I'd be faster than you, Annie." He gulped down a lungful of air. "You still have some growing to do."

Pulling to a halt, Annie fell to her knees into the snow, panting. "But I wasn't far behind. I almost had you."

Walking over, Toby nodded, then held out a hand to help her up. "Yes, you did good. You're getting faster every day."

"You truly think so?" Annie asked, gazing up into his smiling face. "Truly truly?"

Toby laughed, and his chocolate-brown eyes shone with warmth. "Yes, Annie, truly truly." He kept tossing his hat in the air, catching it a mere second before it hit the snow. "But why do you want to be faster than me?"

Annie shrugged. "It looks like fun." She regarded him curiously. "Don't you always try to outrun Phin? He's older and taller than you, but still you race him. Why do you try if you know you won't win?"

Toby shrugged at the mention of his older brother. "Well, I don't *know* I won't win. It's unlikely that I will, but not impossible." Again, he shrugged before once more tossing his hat in the air as high as he could. "So I keep racing him, and perhaps one day I'll win. Perhaps one day I'll best him."

Annie couldn't quite understand Toby when it came to this competitiveness between the two brothers; however, that didn't matter. If it was important to Toby, it was important to her. It was as simple as that. "And that's why I race you," she decided. "To help you practice."

A warm smile lit up his face. "That is so kind of you, Annie. Thank you." Again, his hat flew up in the air, but this time a strong, icy wind caught a hold of it and carried it off.

Toby's eyes widened as he stared at his woolen hat, dancing through the air until it caught on a barren branch of an oak tree high above the ground. "Oh, no." His voice was faint as he trudged through the snow, closer to the tree. "Mother will be furious. She specifically told me not to lose this one, too."

Indeed, Toby had lost, torn or otherwise ruined countless hats while Annie had lost, torn or otherwise ruined countless ribbons. "Then let's get it down," she suggested and marched closer to the tree, her eyes travelling upward along the branches.

"I can't."

Turning around, Annie saw Toby shake his head as he stared at the tree as though it were a giant meant to do him harm. His face had gone pale, and his hands balled into fists. "I can't."

"I'll get it," Annie offered with a shrug.

Toby shook his head. "No, you can't."

"Why not?"

"Because...because..." Toby's mouth closed and opened a couple of times as he squinted against the brilliant winter sun, trying to figure out what he wanted to say. "My father always says a gentleman is to look out for a lady." He glanced at the tree, and a shiver went through him. "You're a lady. You're not meant to look after me. I'm meant to look after you."

Annie frowned, never in her life had she heard such nonsense. "I'm not a lady, Toby," she told him, hands on her hips. "I'm your friend, and we look after each other." She reached out and grasped his hand. "All right?"

Inhaling a deep breath, Toby once more glanced up at his hat, then nodded. "All right. But you need to promise me to be careful, Annie."

"I promise," Annie vowed and then turned to the tree. "Give me a hand, will you?"

Linking his hands, Toby gave her a push so Annie could reach the first, low-hanging branch, pulling herself up, feet braced against the trunk.

"Careful, Annie."

"Don't worry." Pulling herself up onto the branch, Annie held on to the trunk and then pushed to her feet, reaching higher for the next. Step by step, she made her way up the barren branches, unobstructed by the tree's usually dense foliage. "I'm almost there." Only one more branch and she reached out her hand to grab Toby's hat. Her fingertips were almost touching it. "Only a little farther."

"Annie, careful!" Toby called the moment Annie tipped forward. Her feet slipped off the branch below as her right hand grasped another one higher up. For a heart-stopping moment, her feet dangled in the air, her body suspended by her right hand alone.

Below, she heard Toby suck in a sharp breath. He called out to her, but she couldn't answer, her main focus on holding on as panic slowly snuck into her heart. What was she to do now?

And then her hand began to slip. "Toby!"

"Hold on, Annie!"

"I can't!" And then she was falling, her eyes pinched shut in terror.

When the landing finally came, it was nothing as Annie had

expected it. She'd expected a hard thud, perhaps even broken bones. What happened was a rather soft *plop*!

"Are you all right?" came Toby's panicked voice a moment before Annie felt his hands on her shoulders. Then his pale face and wide open eyes appeared in front of her. Never in her life had she seen him look so terrified.

"I'm all right," Annie confirmed as her eyes ran over her arms and legs, uncertain if she was speaking the truth. All seemed to be fine though.

Then she noticed the heap of snow she had landed in. "Did you do this?"

Still panting, Toby nodded. "I couldn't think of what else to do."

Annie smiled at him, then held out her hand so he would help her up. "This was brilliant, Toby!" She brushed some snow off her coat, then surveyed the heaps of snow Toby had pushed under the tree to soften her fall. "Thank you. You saved me!" Then she flung herself into his arms and hugged him as she had never hugged him before.

"I was so afraid you'd die, Annie," Toby whispered as he held her tightly. "I was so afraid I'd lose you."

Blinking back a tear, Annie stepped back. "You looked out for me," she told him with a deep smile.

Toby nodded. "And you looked out for me." He bent down to pick up his hat that had to have slipped off the branch when Annie had. "As friends do." He grinned at her.

"As friends do," Annie echoed, taking his hat and pulling it back over his head.

Friends.

Forever.

# Chapter One
## A PLAN IS HATCHED

*Barrington House, England, Autumn 1801 (or a variation thereof)*

Barrington House with its tall columns and wide-open land held a special place in Anne's heart. She had spent many wonderful years here as a girl, sliding down the banister in the great hall, catching fireflies at dusk and stealing biscuits from the kitchen. She had loved following the Hawke boys on their adventures, exploring the haunted attic or the gloomy library where a whispered word would echo among the rows upon rows of books. She knew every nook and cranny of this place, and whenever the sun began to set and its golden rays drifted in through the ceiling-tall windows in the salon, Anne could not help but sigh in bliss.

Indeed, Barrington House had always been nothing short of heaven for her.

But not today.

"Is he still looking at me?" Anne asked in a tense whisper, forcing herself not to glance over her shoulder, but to keep her eyes fixed on her two cousins, Louisa and Leonora Beaumont, daughters to the Earl of Whickerton.

Dark-haired Leonora frowned at Anne's pinched expression, then cast a questioning look across the ballroom, crammed with guests at this year's ball. "Who?" she asked, her brows drawing down in concentrated observation.

Her sister laughed, "Well, Lord Gillingham, of course." Unlike Leonora's, Louisa's brows rose in a show of triumph as she met Anne's gaze. "Why are you so intent on escaping his company?" There was a teasing note in her voice, and Anne could not help but feel that her beloved cousin was enjoying watching her squirm much.

Louisa and Leonora-or Lou and Leo as family and friends called them-were like night and day. Anne could not say which of her cousins she liked better for they both had such endearing qualities; unfortunately, they also both possessed the ability to rob her of every bit of patience with but a few well-aimed words.

Leonora was reason personified, always coming up with theories about how and why something happened. She was known to ask a thousand questions when something piqued her interest and was rarely seen without a notebook and pencil in hand. Fortunately, it seemed she had not brought them to tonight's ball.

Louisa, on the other hand, often acted on impulse, rarely taking the time to think things through, which frequently aggravated Leonora. Still, Louisa had a way of seeing the truth regardless of its trappings and she never feared to speak her mind, her exuberance intoxicating.

Anne sighed, knowing that neither one of her cousins would accept a half-truth. "Well, he...he simply makes me...uncomfortable," she finally admitted, tucking a stray curl of her dark brown tresses back in place.

"Why?" Leonora asked with a frown as she once more squinted her eyes, no doubt running them over Lord Gillingham to determine the problem. "Is it his breath? Does he smell odd? Does he have sweaty palms?" She glanced down at Anne's gloved hands. "However, that shouldn't affect you. Does he spit when he speaks? Or-?"

"He wants to marry her," Louisa threw in with a sideways eye roll at her sister. Then her inquisitive, green eyes settled back on Anne. "Does he not?"

Anne heaved a deep sigh, "He didn't say as much, but...every time he looks at me I cannot help but feel that..." Her voice trailed off. "What do I do?"

"So, he has neither bad breath nor sweaty palms?" Leonora enquired for knowledge's sake.

Anne shook her head. "Not that I noticed."

"Then why do you object to him?" Again, Leonora ran her eyes over the admittedly dashing lord. "He is tall with thick hair and a symmetrical face. He comports himself with elegance and dances with the necessary proficiency. As far as I know, his family possesses a sizable fortune as well as a reputation free from scandal." Her mouth closed and she blinked, her blue eyes moving to meet Anne's. "Where is your objection?"

Anne shrugged. "I don't know." However, whenever Lord Gillingham drew near, there was that part of her deep down that all but told her to run. She could not explain it. It felt like a sense of dread, of reluctance as though she simply was not where she ought to be. As though she was walking in the wrong direction.

"What kind of man do you wish for?" Leonora enquired; her hands moved as though they were reaching for her notebook and pencil, ready to take notes. When she discovered them absent, the look in her eyes was one of deepest regret.

"Oh, *I* can tell you what kind of man she wishes for, dearest Leo," Louisa exclaimed, her lips curled into a smile that made Anne squirm even more. "I can even tell you which gentleman it is who's standing in the way of her seeing Lord Gillingham-or any other-in a favorable light."

While Anne felt her insides twist and turn in dread, wondering what kind of fantastic story Louisa had cooked up this time, Leonora's jaw dropped in curiosity. "Who?"

Louisa smiled devilishly. "Him." Without turning her head, she let her eyes dart to the wide arch through which more and more guests were entering the ballroom.

Holding Louisa's daring gaze, Anne raised her chin, fighting the urge to turn her head.

Leonora, however, did not hesitate for a second. Her head snapped to the side, and a moment later, the hint of a frown began to crease her forehead. "Lord Barrington?"

Anne felt herself pause, then frown. "What? That's ridiculous!"

Louisa rolled her eyes at her sister. "I quite agree. Phineas Hawke is the last man in the world who would capture a woman's attention."

"You truly ought to call him Lord Barrington," Leonora chided. "It's a question of respect. After all, he inherited his father's title more than four years ago."

Louisa shrugged off her sister's comment as though it were a ludicrous demand that did not make the slightest sense.

While Anne had grown up with the Hawke brothers, their families' country estates closely situated, Louisa and Leonora had only occasionally spent time in their company. However, for Louisa, that had been enough to come to detest the eldest Hawke brother Phineas; and it seemed the feeling was mutual. "No, I meant Mr. Tobias Hawke," Louisa clarified with a smile in Anne's direction. Then she turned and her eyes sought out the man in question.

"Toby?" Anne exclaimed, wondering how on earth Louisa had come to that conclusion. "You must be jesting." Her gaze followed Louisa's and she found herself looking at her childhood friend. As though he felt her looking at him, his head rose, and a second later, his chocolate-brown eyes found hers. A small smile touched his lips, and he winked at her.

"See?" Louisa exclaimed in triumph. "You cannot tell me that he means nothing to you."

Anne stared at her cousin in utter confusion. "Of course not. Why would you think that? He's my dearest friend. Of course, he means something to me."

Louisa crossed her arms over her chest and regarded Anne in that way of hers that said she didn't believe a word Anne was saying.

"Truly," Anne insisted. "He's my friend and nothing more. To me, he'll always be *Little Toby*, the boy who pulled on my braids and hid frogs in my bed." Still, she could not help but smile at the memory, for she'd gotten back at him by hiding his homework, which had gotten him in trouble with his tutor. Toby had been furious when he'd realized it had been her, and he hadn't simply misplaced it.

"Well, he's not *Little Toby* any longer," Louisa remarked with a sideways glance at Tobias's tall stature, "and neither are you *Little Annie*." Her green eyes became thoughtful for a moment before she took a step toward Anne. "I dare you, dear cousin, to look at Tobias not as the boy you knew but as the man you could marry."

Anne's heart stumbled in her chest. "Marry?" she exclaimed, not certain if in horror or something other; something she couldn't quite name. "I could never marry him!"

"Why not?" Leonora interjected curiously, her watchful eyes going back and forth between Anne and her sister. "I must admit that he, too, possesses most amiable qualities. Judging from both your characters, I'd say the two of you would suit."

Louisa rolled her eyes at her sister yet again. "Marriage is not a science experiment, Leo," she snapped, then sighed before a slow smile spread over her face. "It should be about passion. You should choose someone who sets your blood on fire and steals your breath away." Her smile deepened as she looked at her sister. "Have you learned nothing from Mother and Father?"

Indeed, Anne's aunt and uncle had gone against convention, against their parents' wishes and gotten married because they'd been in love. And even today, after thirty years of marriage and six children, they still looked at one another like love-sick youths.

It was...inspiring?

"Lou, I don't disagree with your notion of passion in marriage," Anne stated, "however, Toby is my friend. He's like a brother to me. I could never marry him."

Louisa laughed, "A brother?" Her gaze moved to her sister and then back to Anne. "Well, considering you don't have a brother, I can understand that you have no frame of reference. Still-"

"You're beginning to sound like Leo," Anne pointed out with no small measure of enjoyment.

Louisa rolled her eyes in annoyance. "Don't try to distract me, for it will not work. I love you dearly, and I will not see you married to a man who will no doubt make you miserable. You need to follow your heart in all truly important endeavors, or you'll come to regret it."

"But my heart tells me that-"

"Does it?" Louisa challenged. "Truly? Or have you simply never looked at Tobias in any other way but through the eyes of the little girl you once were?" Her eyes lit up. "In fact, I dare you to look at him right here, right now, and see him as a man grown, not as a boy." She came to stand at Anne's side, her gaze pointed across the ballroom to where Toby and his brother were conversing with a group of gentlemen. "Look at him," she whispered in Anne's ear, "and ask yourself if you truly see him as *Little Toby* still."

Anne drew in a shuddering breath, reluctant to do as her cousin bid her. Still, her gaze moved over her childhood friend, and she knew that she loved him. She loved that teasing spark in his dark brown eyes. She loved the way his gaze strayed to hers every so often. She loved the confidence that existed between them. Always had she known his secrets. Always had he confided in her as she had confided in him. His smile warmed her heart and made her feel special as though it was for her alone.

She loved him.

But did that mean she was *in love* with him?

Clearing her throat, Anne turned to look at her cousin. "I don't know what you hope to accomplish, Lou, but Toby is my friend. He's always been my friend, and-"

"He could be your friend and your husband," Louisa pointed out. "One does not exclude the other." Her gaze narrowed. "Have you ever kissed him?"

Anne's eyes flew open. "Of course not!" The thought alone was ludicrous...wasn't it?

"Well, then I think you should," Louisa stated, "to..." she paused and cast a somewhat annoyed look at her sister, "to test your theory."

Leonora's face brightened at the thought of an experiment. "Indeed, a kiss would prove quite telling in determining how you feel about him. It will certainly tell you whether or not you love him as a brother." Again, her fingers moved as though they longed to grasp that elusive pencil and jot down the parameters of Louisa's proposed experiment.

Panic welled up in Anne's heart, and she shook her head vehemently. "You're mad!" she exclaimed in a hushed voice, looking from one cousin to the other. "You cannot truly suggest I walk up to him and kiss him? I'd be ruined!" More than that, it would forever alter the friendship between them. If she kissed him, they could never be *Little Toby* and *Little Annie* again. What if she lost him?

The thought was too terrifying to bear!

"You're right on that account," Leonora pointed out reasonably, the tip of her forefinger tapping against her lips as she thought. "We need some kind of pretext."

"How about a mistletoe kiss?" Louisa suggested, wiggling her brows as she looked at Anne.

Anne huffed out an annoyed breath. "It's not Christmas."

"It will be soon," the two sisters said as one. Why was it that the second her cousins finally found some common ground, it was to her disadvantage?

"The Archibald Christmas house party is not far off," Leo pointed out, her eyes slightly squinted as she no doubt counted out the days.

Louisa's face brightened. "I like how you think, Sister." Now, that was a first!

"You cannot be serious," Anne stated feebly, getting the disquieting feeling that no matter what she said she could not win this.

Smiling gently, Louisa reached out to tuck another stray curl behind Anne's ear. "Listen, you know that I'm right even if you cannot admit it right now. You care for him, and you need to know how much before you make a decision to marry anyone." Her green eyes were soft and kind, and Anne knew that despite Louisa's tendency to push people into something they did not want to do, her actions sprang from a deep sense of concern. She cared, deeply, and Anne loved her for it.

"What if...?" Anne began, not certain what it was she wanted to ask.

"If the kiss makes you think of *Little Toby* hiding frogs in your bed," Louisa said with a smirk, "then you laugh it off and continue your friendship as before. If, however," her cousin's gaze grew imploring, "it makes you want to swoon into his arms and never let go, then I think it's fair to say that you do not see him as a brother."

"I agree with that assessment," Leonora threw in, an equally sympathetic smile on her face as she stood shoulder to shoulder with her sister, her clear blue eyes looking into Anne's.

Not knowing what to say, Anne stared at her two beloved cousins. She could not deny that what they said made sense; however, there was one aspect neither one of them had considered yet. What if Tobias would forever see *her* as *Little Annie*? What if their kiss would prove that she loved him, but he would forever see her as the little sister who'd discovered his secret hiding place for the biscuits they'd stolen from the kitchen and eaten them all? What if Tobias could never see anything more in her?

What if kissing him would break her heart?

# Chapter Two

## A DISASTER WAITING TO HAPPEN

*Near Windmere Park, England, December 1801 (or a variation thereof)*
*A few days before Christmas*

Anne was tempted to throw herself out of the moving carriage. No doubt, the heaps of snow covering the countryside would dampen her fall, allowing her to emerge from such an admittedly drastic measure unscathed. Then she could pick herself up, dust herself off and begin walking back the way they'd come.

Back home.

Away from Windmere Park.

Away from Louisa and Leonora.

Away from...Tobias.

Admittedly, she might freeze to death; however, at present, Anne couldn't say that the thought bothered her overly much. Indeed, any place seemed preferable to being locked up in a moving carriage with her two *beloved* cousins as well as their snoozing grandmother on her way to Windmere Park, Lord Archibald's Christmas house party and all that it entailed looming in her future. Why on earth had she agreed to attend? She had to have been mad; after all, this couldn't end in anything else but utter disaster.

Louisa and Leonora would make certain of that.

"How soon would you say we perform this experiment?" Leonora asked her sister as she tapped the back of her pencil on the notebook in her lap. "I do not believe it wise to rush things."

Seated next to a squirming Anne, Louisa laughed, "Oh, I wouldn't mind pushing them both under the mistletoe the moment we arrive." She grinned at Anne's shocked expression. "The sooner, the better."

Leonora frowned. "It ought not be too obvious," she pointed out. "After all, no one ought to know what we're about. If indeed Anne realizes she sees him as a brother, it needs to be clear that the only reason they kissed was because they happened to end up under the mistletoe. Nothing more."

"Should we make a wager?" Louisa suggested with a wide, wicked grin, her strawberry blond curls tucked under a fur-lined hood. "Brother or no brother?"

Leonora frowned. "Ladies are not to wager," she pointed out; still, a hint of intrigue rang in her voice.

Anne heaved a deep sigh. "Would it make any difference if I objected to this?" she asked, looking from one cousin to the other.

"To the wager or the experiment?" Leonora asked to clarify.

"Both."

Louisa shook her head, laughing. "Not in the slightest. After all, you agreed to this."

"Did I?" Anne asked with a frown. "I don't recall that I did. What I do recall is objecting to this from the start."

Pencil balanced between two fingers, Leonora placed the tip of her forefinger on her lips, her blue eyes thoughtful. "She's right," she told her sister. "She never agreed."

Louisa shrugged. "A minor detail." She grinned at Anne. "One to be neglected. Now," her gaze moved back to Leonora, "how do we do this? I'm willing to wait a day or two, but that's all I'm willing to concede." She eagerly rubbed her hands together, a gesture that made her look almost villainous. "If we can't push them, then we need to lure Tobias." She looked at Anne. "You'll be waiting under the mistletoe, and we'll make up some excuse to send him your way."

Anne was about to object-again!-when Leo stilled, pencil frozen in mid-air. "What if, before Tobias can reach her side, another gentleman happens to step under the mistletoe with her?"

Louisa frowned, clearly displeased to have a flaw pointed out in her plan. "Then we simply have to time it well." She looked at Anne. "The second you see him move toward you, you step forward and under the mistletoe." She sighed rather exasperatedly, "Seriously, ladies, it cannot be that hard. Countless people get kissed under a sprig of mistletoe every year."

Leonora nodded. "Yes, but perhaps not by the right person." Her blue gaze shifted to Anne. "I hear Lord Gillingham will be in attendance as well."

Anne groaned...without knowing why. After all, the young lord was perfectly amiable. There was no good reason for her to dislike him.

"Very well," Louisa exclaimed, her gaze moving from Anne to Leo and back. "This is what we'll do. Anne, you wait near a conveniently situated mistletoe. Leo, you then fetch Tobias while I make certain that no other gentleman interferes."

Leonora frowned. "How?"

"I don't know," Louisa replied with a nonchalant shrug, not the slightest hint of doubt or concern in her voice. "I'll think of something. If I must, I'll trip them."

For a second, Leonora looked horrified, her gaze momentarily darting to their sleeping grandmother seated beside her, before she inhaled a deep breath-clearly, her sister's exaggerations were nothing new to her-and asked, "What would you say is a conveniently situated mistletoe?" The tip of her pencil came to rest on a blank page in her notebook, ready to jot down notes.

Unfortunately, Louisa merely shrugged. "I'll know it when I see it."

Leonora sighed in disappointment.

Leaning back in her seat, Anne looked out the window as she spotted a large estate on the horizon. It sat snugly surrounded by tall-growing trees on one side and wide open expanse on the other. Powdery snowflakes drifted down to settle upon the evergreen trees standing like sentinels around the cream-colored estate, its darker roof in stark contrast to the white landscape. The path leading up to the front of the house snaked in wide curves through the snowy blanket around them, and Anne spotted another carriage a little way ahead of them.

No doubt Lord Archibald's house party would once again be well-attended, and the thought of countless people witnessing what would no doubt be one of the most embarrassing moments of her life made Anne contemplate flinging herself out of the moving carriage once again.

"Don't even think about it!" Louisa warned, her eyes oddly penetrating as she looked at Anne.

Frowning, Anne turned to her cousin with an innocent face. "What? What are you talking about?"

"I can see what you're thinking," Louisa stated with confidence. "You're thinking of running off, which is why I feel compelled to tell you that you won't succeed." A warm smile spread over her face before she reached out and gently patted Anne's hand. "Don't worry. We're only doing this to help you."

Anne sighed. "I simply don't think-"

"Fine, try this," Louisa interrupted. "Close your eyes and-" Her brows drew together in disapproval. "Close your eyes!" When Anne finally complied, she continued, "Now, imagine you're standing in front of Lord Gillingham."

A shudder shook Anne, but she forced her eyes to remain closed, knowing she would never hear the end of it if she didn't.

"Now, picture him smiling at you, taking your hand," Louisa whispered, her voice now soft and oddly melodious as though she sought to lull Anne into a deep slumber. Unfortunately, with the image of Lord Gillingham in mind, Anne couldn't bring herself to relax. "Now, he's leaning down, his lips aiming for yours and-"

"Ugh!" Anne couldn't help it for the thought made her queasy. Her eyes flew open and she shook her head.

Again, Louisa's brows rose in triumph. "I think that's very telling." She looked at Leonora. "Don't you?"

Leonora nodded in agreement before she lowered her gaze to the notebook in her lap and began to write. "Indeed, that was very telling. A quite forceful reaction if I may say so."

"Now, to compare," Louisa continued, her green eyes sparkling as she looked at Anne. "Picture Tobias standing in front of you, holding your hand and-" When Anne failed to react, Louisa's brows rose. "Well?"

"I was just thinking how sad it is that your family fell ill so short before Christmas," Anne lamented perhaps a bit too forcefully. "Your parents always enjoyed the Archibald house party, and poor Grandma Edie." She looked at the peacefully snoozing woman. Although of small stature, Grandma Edie was a force of nature, a no-nonsense kind of woman, who spoke her mind whenever it pleased her and turned a deaf ear just as often. "It must be hard to be away from home at such an advanced age, especially around Christmas. Will your family not miss you all?How will they make do without you?" She looked from one cousin to the other.

Leonora's pencil paused, and her gaze rose. "Oh, they'll be fine. Jules will see to them as she always does." Indeed, the eldest Beaumont sister had all but taken on the role of companion for their elderly grandmother. She was the heart and soul of the family, always seeing to everyone and ensuring that all was well.

"But you already know this," Louisa told Anne, a knowing look in her watchful eyes.. "Therefore, it is only too obvious that you only seek to distract us with your concern." She glanced at her grandmother. "Grandma Edie will enjoy the diversion and I'm sure Jules will cherish not playing the companion for a little while. There, happy now?"

Anne grinned sheepishly. "A girl can try, can't she?"

Louisa chuckled, "I suppose that's true. Now," she reached out and brushed a hand over Anne's face, urging her to close her eyes. "Simply... think of him."

Sighing, Anne leaned back in her seat, determined to think of anyone but Tobias. However, her wayward thoughts wouldn't comply, and she found herself remembering the first ball after her coming out. She'd been terrified by the crush of people, like a gazelle watching a stampede heading its way.

And then Tobias had appeared out of nowhere. He'd taken her hand in his and pulled her onto the dance floor. "Look at me," he'd whispered with that endearing half-smile curling his lips, "and breathe. They're more afraid of you than you are of them."

Anne had laughed then, and the tense knot inside her had come undone. She'd been able to breathe, comforted by the warmth in his chocolate-brown eyes and the way his hand held onto hers, a reassuring pressure, assuring her that she wasn't alone.

That he was there.

And always would be.

Indeed, she loved him. She loved him with all her heart and soul. Anne had always known that. But...was she *in love* with him? Was that possible without her even noticing?

That night, Tobias had not left her side, his presence a safe anchor. They'd laughed and teased each other and then retreated behind a long row of tall, potted plants, secretly poking fun at the most snobbish of ladies to walk by their hiding place.

And then, shortly before midnight, there'd been a moment when Tobias had looked at her, his brown eyes warm and lingering, before he'd reached out, catching a stray curl of hers between his fingertips. He'd gazed at it in a deeply stirring way and then slowly tucked it back behind her ear, the tips of his fingers gently brushing against her skin.

Anne had barely been able to breathe in that moment, an odd sensation dancing across her skin that she could not help but wonder about now. She remembered it well. It had been a moment that had been burnt into her memory...but why? Would she have welcomed a kiss then and there? Or would she have refused him, certain that he was a brother to her and nothing more?

Cursing her meddlesome cousins, Anne realized as the carriage finally pulled to a halt that a part of her did want to kiss Tobias after all.

Indeed, curiosity suddenly surged through her, making her wonder what it would feel like to have him look at her again as he had then. To feel him move closer? To feel his hands on hers? And...and...?

Nevertheless, the thought of kissing Tobias with Heaven knew how many witnesses watching them with hawk's eyes still turned Anne's stomach. What she wanted was to be alone with him, to retreat behind a row of potted plants, invisible to the world, and see nothing and no one but him.

Unfortunately, knowing her cousins, Anne was certain that she wouldn't get her wish.

# Chapter Three

## FRIENDS OF OLD

Tobias Hawke, second son to the late Viscount Barrington, stood in the entryway of Windmere Park like a fool and stared at his childhood friend, Miss Anne Thatcher, as she and her two cousins climbed out of their carriage.

Snowflakes, sparkling like diamonds, drifted down to settle in her mahogany tresses. Still, they could never outshine the glow in her deep azure gaze, warm, and yet, deeply stirring as they swept over their destination. The moment they fell on Tobias, the air seemed to thin, and for a second, he feared his heart would stop. Then a dazzling smile claimed her lips, and she looked at him in that way that was uniquely hers.

As though her day had brightened now that they were back together.

As though she had longed to see him ever since their last meeting.

As though her heart beat as fast as his own.

"You're staring, Brother," Phineas hissed beside him, a teasing chuckle following his observation.

Clearing his throat, Tobias forced his gaze away from her, then shifted on his feet to look at his brother. "I'm merely happy to see her again. It's been a while. That is all."

Phineas had always possessed a devilish streak, his eyes such a dark shade of brown that they seemed almost black, giving him a bit of a wicked allure, at least as far as young debutantes were concerned. Tobias, however, would have preferred a less roguish brother for Phineas enjoyed nothing more than seeing him squirm.

Lately, it had become his brother's most favored pastime.

"Certainly," Phineas replied, his voice dripping with sarcasm, "and Father and Uncle Henry stopped by last night for a game of cards." Laughter rumbled in his chest, and Tobias inhaled a deep breath, willing himself not to respond for it would only spur Phineas on.

Casting his brother a cautioning gaze, Tobias moved toward the three young women as well as the cousins' grandmother, offering a formal bow. Given her advanced age, he was rather surprised the Dowager Lady Whickerton was in attendance; however, he could not deny that there was steel in the way her watchful gaze moved from him to Phineas, whispering of a sharp mind. "I'm delighted to see you are in attendance as well." For a moment, his eyes lingered on Anne and continued to do so for yet a moment longer. Then he rather abruptly turned to the dowager. "Do you remember my brother, Lady Whickerton?" Indeed, who could ever forget?

"Of course, the wicked one," the cousins' grandmother chuckled, her pale eyes sizing up Phineas without difficulty before they briefly came to rest on Lady Louisa. "Have you acquired manners since last we met?"

Phineas laughed. "I thought I had; however, I'm afraid I might have misplaced them once again. I'll inform you immediately should I succeed in locating them."

The dowager chortled. "A wicked one, indeed." Shaking her head, she slowly hobbled toward the front hall, leaning heavily upon her walking stick. "Give me a head start, ladies," she told the three young women over her shoulder. "I'm certain you'll catch up with me at the landing."

"Little Annie," Phineas greeted Anne with a sideways glance at Tobias. "How long has it been? Ten? Twenty years? I must say I hardly recognize you."

Shaking her head at Phineas, Anne still smiled at him and her smile lit up her eyes in a most beautiful way. Tobias couldn't help but dislike his brother for it. "How are you, Phin?"

Winking at her, Phineas cast his brother another sideways glance. "I am fine now that you're here, Annie. I must say I missed you dearly." Tobias wanted to kick him.

Fortunately, Anne merely chuckled and shook her head at him, well-versed in interpreting Phineas's odd comments. "Are you ever serious, Phin?" she asked. "A man of your age should have learnt to comport himself well, should he not?"

Phin frowned. "Are you calling me old?"

"No, simply immature."

His brother laughed. "That, I can live with."

While Lady Leonora frowned at his brother, Lady Louisa looked ready to strangle him. "I had not realized," Lady Louisa began, open censure in her voice, "that you would accompany your brother to this house party. I'd heard you had decided to remain in Town."

Cocking his head to the side, Phin regarded her, a touch of amusement visible in the way his lips twitched. "Did you now? Well, my dearest Lulu, I must say you sound displeased to see me. Have I done anything to wrong you?" He cast her a sickeningly sweet smile, which made even Tobias want to hit him over the head.

Lady Louisa was fuming, "Do not call me that!" she hissed as she stepped toward him, her chin raised and her eyes shooting fire. "I've told you so before, and I'm saying it again. I am not a poodle, and you're not to call me that! Is that clear?" Before Phin could answer, she spun on her heel and marched inside, Lady Leonora following on her heel.

"Was that truly necessary?" Anne chided him. "You used to be such a charming boy."

Phin chuckled, "What can I say? Your cousin brings out the best side of me."

Anne shook her head at him. "You truly ought to apologize, *Lord Barrington*." Her brows rose and, to his utter surprise, Tobias found his brother sigh and then hasten after the two sisters.

He looked at Anne. "This won't end well," he told her, offering her his arm. His own began to tingle when she slipped her hand through, her breath brushing over his cheek as she turned to speak to him.

"I suppose there are two possible outcomes," she said with a chuckle. "Either my cousin kills him in a fit of anger before the year is out or..." She stopped in her tracks, and her deep blue eyes looked up into his as though looking for something.

"Or?" Tobias asked, overwhelmed by her sudden nearness after almost a month apart. Had it truly been that long?

Anne drew in a bit of a shuddering breath. "Or they'll fall madly in love with one another." Her words hung between them as they stood in the entry hall and looked at one another.

Tobias swallowed. "I admit I'm hoping for the second possibility for despite his shortcomings I'm rather fond of my brother."

"You admit it openly?" Anne teased, that smile of hers once more melting his heart.

Tobias laughed, although the sound did come out a bit strangled. "Well, he is my brother and, although I hate to admit it, he's also my best friend."

A teasing frown played over her face. "I thought *I* was your best friend. After all, I know all your secrets."

Except one, Tobias thought, wondering how Anne would react if she ever learned what he thought about when he looked at her. "Indeed, you are," he assured her. "Especially when Phin is acting particularly boorish. Then, there's truly no competition." Sighing, he marveled at the strange stirrings in his heart when those deep blue eyes looked into his own. "You'll always be the dearest friend I'll ever have, Annie." The moment the words left his lips, Tobias could have kicked himself. Although he hadn't lied, he had to admit that he no longer saw her as the friend she'd once been to him...and the thought that *she* might think of him thus was utterly disheartening.

For a second, her smile seemed to falter before it returned with greater force. "Well, so long as we remain the best of friends, I shall have nothing to complain about."

*But I do,* Tobias thought the moment her eyes moved from his to look over his shoulder. He felt her arm tense and her breath shudder past her lips. "Are you all right?" he asked, noting the tinge of red that came to her cheeks.

When she failed to answer, he turned to look...and instantly wished he hadn't.

Stepping into the entry hall was none other than Lord Gillingham, a polished, sickeningly perfect, young gentleman who seemed to fancy Anne as of late. More than once, Tobias had seen them dance, the young lord's eyes glowing in admiration as he'd smiled down at her.

And every time, Tobias had had to fight the urge to cut in then and there and stake his claim. But he hadn't for he *had* no claim on her.

That was the disheartening truth.

Anne was his friend, certainly; however, beyond that, they had no understanding and, if he never managed to work up the nerve to ask for more, they never would.

Perhaps this house party was the perfect opportunity to broach the subject. But what if she refused him? What if he lost her? After all, she *was* the best friend he'd ever had, and he could not bear the thought of losing all they were to each other.

Always had they stood as one, even as children.

A smile teased his lips as he remembered a hot summer many years ago. They had been no older than ten or eleven and had both been invited to attend his mother's annual garden party as *official guests* as she had told them with a wink. It had been an honor, and it had made them feel grown beyond their years.

As always Phineas had not been impressed at all; instead, he had concocted a plan to ruin his little brother's big day. With a ruse, Phin had lured him to the lake and then shoved him in, soaking Tobias's elegant wardrobe.

He'd looked like a drowned rat.

As though to make amends, Phineas had offered to guide him back into the house unseen so Tobias could change. He had, however, led him straight into the arriving guests' path.

Tobias could still remember the sound of their approach as he had stood in the hall, dripping onto the floor, their footsteps echoing along the parquet on the other side of the door.

Closer and closer.

Tobias had been frozen to the spot, unable to move, tears starting to brim in his eyes.

And then he'd spotted Annie near the garden doors, her eyes wide as she had stared at him, her gaze gliding over his soaked clothing.

What had happened then would forever be burned into Tobias's memory.

With a swiftness her dress shouldn't have allowed for, Annie had moved toward him the second the entrance door had swung open, allowing in the guests. He could still feel her little hand as she had shoved him aside, then darted into the hall and pulled to a halt at the last second.

The moment the guests took note of her, her eyes rolled back in her head and she had collapsed onto the floor in one of the best feigned faints Tobias had seen to this day, giving him the time he had needed to slink upstairs and change.

Never would Tobias forget what she had done for him. How she had stood by him, no questions asked. After all, she was his friend, his best friend, and he could not imagine a life without her by his side. Could he risk addressing his regard for her? How it had changed over the course of the last year?

Would it be worth it?

# Chapter Four

## A DEDICATED COUSIN

"He's an insufferable…!" For a short moment, words failed Louisa. Then, however, something wicked sparked in her eyes and she instantly clamped her lips shut to contain the no doubt highly inappropriate comparisons that now lay on the tip of her tongue.

"Who?" Leonora asked as the three of them ventured through the downstairs rooms. Everything glowed in red and gold, and the smell of fresh-cut evergreens lingered in the air, mingling with the delicious aromas of hot tea and warm pastries as well as the smoky tinge of lit firewood, earthy and fresh. Ice crystals clung to the outside of the windowpanes, and the soft glow of the snow made everything look unbelievably peaceful.

"Who?" Louisa gasped, incredulity in her eyes as her hands rose to settle on her hips. "Have you even been listening to a word I've said?"

Blinking, Leonora sighed and then looked up from the notebook in her hand, which held a rough sketch of Windmere Park's ground floor. "Pardon?" she mumbled before her gaze moved over the room once more. Then her fingers twitched, and a moment later, she made a small X on the page, marking the doorway leading into the drawing room, where a handful of guests had assembled, discussing their plans for later that day.

Louisa rolled her eyes. Then her shoulders slumped and she looked at Anne. "I cannot help but wonder how two brothers can be so vastly different. While one is charming and kind and utterly handsome," Anne could not deny that her heart skipped a beat at the thought of Tobias, "the other is...is the devil incarnate." Louisa huffed out an exasperated breath before she suddenly stilled and a deeply concerning smile came to her lips. "Do you think it's possible that that devilish man is not who he claims to be? Perhaps he's an impostor. Or he was adopted. Or the late Lady Barrington had an affair and that devilish man is not the late lord's true son." She shrugged, clearly taken with the idea. "It could be anything."

Anne chuckled, taking one of Louisa's hands into her own. "Whether you like it or not, I'm afraid Phineas is who he says he is. After all, I've grown up with him. He's never been different."

Louisa's shoulders slumped, and she all but glared at Anne for destroying her hopes. "But there has to be a reason? Tobias is so...so... and that brother of his is..." She grimaced, then shook herself.

Anne laughed, grateful for this small distraction. Perhaps there was a way to dissuade her cousins from shoving her and Tobias under a sprig of mistletoe by ensuring that Louisa's thoughts were focused on something else.

Or rather someone else.

And Phineas proved to be quite captivating for Lou!

"There," Leonora exclaimed as she turned to face them, the faraway expression gone from her eyes. "I think I've got them all."

This time, it was Louisa who frowned. "All of what?"

Leonora paused, her eyes darting to the sketch in her notebook and then back up to her sister. "The sprigs of mistletoe. I've taken down all the locations...as we discussed." She stepped closer and turned the book in her hands to show the other two what she'd noted down. "Of course, most are found in highly frequented areas, in doorways as well as near the pianoforte. Which one would you say is the one most conveniently placed?" she asked her sister.

Anne sighed, "I'm telling you here and now, I will not step under one of those dreadful things with a dozen people around to stare at me." Her brows rose for emphasis as she looked from one cousin to the other.

Louisa chuckled, "You sound as though you agree to our plan," she pointed out. "And here I thought you were opposed to the whole idea. Has seeing Tobias changed your mind?" She wiggled her brows for good measure.

Anne paused. *Had it?*

Indeed, seeing Tobias again after almost a month apart had stirred something within her. She'd barely been able to keep her eyes off him, off that teasing smile, off those chocolate-brown eyes that seemed to see right through her. They'd touched no more than was considered appropriate, and yet, the feel of his arm under her hand had all but stolen her breath. What did this mean? Had she truly come to care for him beyond the measurements of their friendship? Or was she simply feeling self-conscious at the thought of a mistletoe kiss with him?

"Oh, look, Leo, she's blushing!" Louisa observed delightedly before she turned to her sister. "I think we have our answer right here."

"Great!" Anne cried, seizing this opportunity. "Then we don't need that dreadful mistletoe kiss after all. I-"

"Oh, no! You're not getting out of this." Shaking her head at her, Louisa chuckled, "Why are you so reluctant? I should think you'd want to know how you feel about him."

"I do know how I feel about him," Anne hastened to assure her meddlesome cousin.

"Truly?" Louisa asked with a doubtful look in her green eyes.

Anne sighed, "Perhaps." Her spirits sank as her short-lived hopes fell into the dust at her feet. "But why now? Why here?"

"Why not?" Louisa countered. "Are you not worried that he might agree to a match elsewhere if he thinks you indifferent? Has that not ever crossed your mind? After all, he's got his father's title to consider."

"You mean, his brother's," Leonora corrected.

Louisa rolled her eyes, ignoring her sister's objection. "He might need to father an heir and-"

"Lord Barrington needs an heir," Leonora corrected once again, her frown deepening. "You do know how this works, do you not?"

Louisa's nose crinkled as though she smelled something rotten. "That man is a disgrace, and I do not believe for a second that he'll ever find a woman foolish enough to marry him." She scoffed, "The thought alone is ludicrous. No, after that man's no doubt untimely passing, Tobias will need to assume the title and provide an heir. Therefore-"

"That is quite harsh!" Leonora objected. "It is poor form to speak of him thusly."

Anne nodded, unable to hide the grin that stole onto her face. "Indeed, if I didn't know any better, I'd say...*you* liked him."

Louisa's jaw dropped; however, she quickly recovered, her eyes narrowing. "You must be mad! I hate that man. No, *hate* is not a strong enough word. I loathe that man."

"Why?" Anne asked simply. "What on earth has he ever done to you?"

Louisa's lips clamped shut. *Now, this looked promising!*

"It cannot simply be because he calls you Lulu."

Her cousin's nostrils flared, but for once in her life, Louisa remained quiet. Very telling! Very telling, indeed.

"I agree," Leonora threw in, earning herself a dark glare from her sister. "Even taking your effervescent character into account, I cannot imagine that anyone would be riled in such a way by a simple dislike to a nickname."

"Indeed," Anne chimed in, enjoying that it was finally Louisa's turn to squirm. "Therefore, I assume that you do like him for your reaction is as telling as mine." Anne swallowed hard when she realized what she'd just admitted to.

Of course, her slip of the tongue had not escaped Louisa, whose face instantly brightened. "I was right!" she declared triumphantly. "You *do* like him."

"Perhaps," Anne croaked.

"Would you stop saying that?" Louisa huffed, a hint of exhaustion coming to her features. "Why can't you simply admit that you care for him? He clearly adores you. Why are you so afraid to kiss him?"

"Why are you so certain he's the one for me?" Anne countered in a hushed voice, worried that someone might overhear as they were standing in the hall with new guests coming and going every now and then.

"Very well," Louisa said after a long breath. "I admit I'm growing tired of this discussion. So, how about this? You kiss Tobias under some mistletoe, and if I'm right, if he actually is the one for you and you end up marrying him, then I promise I'll kiss...that man." Her jaw tightened, but she did not drop her gaze.

"You'll kiss Phin?" Anne asked, staring at her cousin.

"Yes."

"Under some mistletoe?"

Louisa shrugged. "I don't care. Wherever you like."

Anne felt her eyes go round before she looked at Leonora, who appeared equally shocked. "You heard her say it, too; didn't you?"

Leonora nodded. "Are you serious?" she asked her sister. "Why would you agree to kiss someone you detest?"

"Because I want to see her happy," Louisa told her sister with a sideways glance at Anne, "and I'm convinced she'll never be happy with another. As I'm unable to convince her of it, I suppose this is the only way to get her to agree." She turned to Anne, holding out her hand. "Do we have a deal?"

Swallowing, Anne stared at her cousin. "You'd do that for me?"

Louisa smiled at her. "Of course. I may not appear as the most compassionate person, but I do love you, dear cousin, and I want to see you matched with the man who holds your heart." She sighed, "If you believe nothing else, can you at least believe that?"

Blinking back tears, Anne nodded. Then she grasped Louisa's hand. "Deal."

With rather unblinking eyes, Leonora looked back and forth between them. "I think we could all do with a bit of a distraction. Do you not agree?"

Both nodded before Louisa smiled that rather disconcerting smile of hers. "Perfect because I believe I just glimpsed Lord Gillingham enter the drawing room."

Anne barely managed to stifle the groan that wanted to escape her lips. “Well, then, let’s have some tea. I admit I’m rather parched.”

Louisa snickered before she drew Anne’s arm through the crook of hers, and the three of them headed down the corridor to join the other guests as well as Grandma Edie in the drawing room.

Oh, dear, what had she just agreed to?

# Chapter Five

## SIMPLY KISS THE GIRL

The sound of laughter echoed up the stairs to the first floor as Tobias and his brother left their chambers and made to head downstairs to join the other guests. Was Anne among them? Tobias wondered. At the thought of seeing her, his heart skipped a beat. Had it always done that? Had he simply never noticed? Or had something changed over the course of the past year?

Ever since that ball when they'd hidden together behind that row of potted plants, something had been different.

Felt different.

"I've glimpsed at least three sprigs of mistletoe thus far," Phineas remarked with a chuckle as they made their way downstairs. "Would I be wrong to assume that you do not have any immediate plans of collecting a few kisses? At least not by a variety of ladies?" His brows rose inquisitively as he looked at Tobias.

"Why would you assume that?" Admittedly, the thought of kissing Anne was overwhelmingly enchanting! Of course, beyond that, his brother was right.

Phineas chuckled, "Do you truly need me to say it, Brother?" They stepped off the last stair and turned toward the drawing room. Stopping in the doorway, Phineas leaned in conspiratorially. "A blind man could see how utterly besotted you are with our little Annie."

Tobias cringed at his brother's observation-not that he could fault it, for his gaze instantly found and settled upon the enchanting woman with the deep blue eyes who'd been nothing more than his dearest friend since the day they'd first met.

Now, however, he felt his palms grow moist with nervous excitement at the thought of addressing her. Not long ago, they'd conversed with such ease about every subject imaginable, and now? Now, it seemed a simple greeting might tie up his tongue.

"Ah!" Phineas exclaimed in a hushed tone. "The competitor!"

"What?" Frowning, Tobias looked at his brother before turning in the direction Phineas indicated with a subtle nod of his head. His eyes fell on Lord Gillingham as he greeted Anne and her cousins, bowing formally to all three ladies. His gaze, however, remained locked on Anne.

Tobias's insides twisted painfully.

"He seems to have taken a special interest in our little Annie," Phineas mumbled with a smirk on his face. "Would you say they're suited to one another?" He turned to look at his brother.

Tobias wanted to kick him. "Why are you doing this?" he hissed under his breath.

Phineas shrugged. "I'm only trying to help you along, dear Brother. After all, there is no point in me pointing out charming ladies to you when your heart has already chosen. Would you not agree?" His brows rose in question.

Gritting his teeth, Tobias remained quiet, uncertain what to do or say. After all, Phineas tended to act without thinking, and the last thing Tobias wanted was for his brother to say something to anyone, least of all to Anne, that Tobias wasn't yet ready to become known.

"Will you at least admit that you no longer see her as our little sister?" Phineas dared him. "You've been talking about little else these past few months. It's always been 'Anne here' and 'Anne there'. Quite frankly, if you don't make up your mind soon and ask for her hand, I'll do it for you."

Tobias didn't know if he wanted to sink into a hole in the ground or stride across the room, toss Anne over his shoulder and carry her off. "What if she doesn't want me?" he whispered, shocking himself by discussing this with his brother of all people. "What if she wants... him?" He all but glared across the drawing room to where Anne was nodding to something Lord Gillingham had said.

"I doubt she does," Phineas replied with a shrug.

"How do you know?"

"Call it a sixth sense. It's in the way she looks at him." He chuckled, "Or rather in the way she doesn't."

Tobias felt his hopes rise. "What do you mean?"

His brother sighed, "Well, she looks at you in the same besotted way as you look at her." Again, he chuckled. "I'd say you're a perfect match."

Tobias sighed, afraid to trust his brother's observational skills. "Honestly, how much can you truly tell from a look? I don't see a difference in how she looks at me and at him." Was that true? Or was he simply afraid to hope that there was?

"Well, if indeed, you're right and she cares for Gillingham," Phineas stated with a tinge of amusement in his voice, "then you have two options." Here, he stopped and wouldn't open his mouth again until Tobias begrudgingly asked him to continue. "One, you can stand by and wait until she agrees to marry Gillingham." Indeed, Tobias had never encountered a thought more terrifying. "Or, two," Phineas turned to meet his brother's gaze, "you could change her mind." A roguish grin spread over his face.

Running a hand through his hair, Tobias tried to think of anything to say that would distract his brother from his current line of thinking. "What about Lady Louisa?" he asked, noting the way she cast bone-chilling glares in Phineas's direction. "What happened between the two of you?"

Grinning at her, his brother shrugged. "Nothing."

"So, she hates you for no reason?"

"I'm certain she has one," Phineas replied, turning to look at Tobias with that utterly innocent expression on his face that made women swoon at his feet without realizing the danger they were putting themselves in. "However, I'm not aware of it."

"Why do you call her Lulu? It seems to rile her."

His brother chuckled, "That is precisely why I do it."

"Pardon me?"

Phineas heaved a somewhat exasperated sigh, "Have you never known the joys that come from fighting with a woman?"

"Joys?" Tobias asked, eyeing his brother through narrowed eyes. "Are you honestly saying that you enjoy her reaction?" He paused. "Do you care for her?"

For a split second, a muscle in Phineas's jaw tensed before he shook his head laughing. "No one can deny that she's a beautiful woman," he stated, that wicked smirk back on his face, "and spirited as well." He shrugged. "Of course, I wouldn't mind stealing a kiss. No one in their right mind would. The lady has a very tempting mouth." His brows wiggled, suggesting the directions of his thoughts-not that they were in doubt. "Perhaps the two of us meeting here this Christmas will provide such an opportunity." He glanced at the sprig of mistletoe hanging near the pianoforte. "Do you think she would slap me if I pulled her under that bit of greenery there and kissed her?" Phineas asked with a chuckle as he looked at the lady in question, completely unimpressed by the hateful glare she sent his way.

Tobias laughed, "Oh, please do so for I do believe the lady will do much worse to you than grant you a simple slap." He grasped his brother's shoulder and met his gaze. "I cannot rightly say that you would not deserve it."

Phineas grinned devilishly. "I admit I'm thoroughly tempted." His eyes moved back to Lady Louisa, and for a terrible moment, Tobias truly thought his brother would stride across the room, drag the lady under the mistletoe dangling near the pianoforte and steal a kiss. Fortunately, Phineas was no fool. He often pretended to be one, but Tobias could see his brother's thoughts churning behind those dark eyes.

Phineas turned back to Tobias. "What about you? Do you think Anne would slap you if you dared to kiss her?"

Tobias cringed.

"Ah!" his brother exclaimed as though he'd just solved a most fascinating riddle. "I see, you've wondered about it yourself."

Swallowing hard, Tobias linked his arms behind his back, trying his utmost not to look at Anne, who was still-to his utter regret-speaking to Lord Gillingham.

Beside him, Phineas sighed, "Simply kiss the girl," he whispered before his black gaze met Tobias's, a wicked gleam coming to his eyes, "or I shall do it for you." His brows went up and down in challenge before he turned and walked away without another word.

Shocked, Tobias stared after him, worried what his brother might do. For although Phineas was no fool, he'd more than once proved to be a rogue of the worst kind.

# Chapter Six

## UNDER THE MISTLETOE

For the life of her, Anne could not find a polite way to rid herself of Lord Gillingham's company. The man had been all but stuck to her side ever since he'd arrived earlier that day. Fate also saw them seated next to one another during supper, refusing to grant Anne a short reprieve.

By the time everyone returned to the drawing room, Anne was exhausted.

"The venison was exquisite," Lord Gillingham commented as they stood near the pianoforte at a safe distance from the nearest sprig of mistletoe. Thanks to Leonora's diligent observations, Anne knew well which areas to avoid. "This has indeed been a splendid evening." He smiled at her, and she could see his blue eyes light up with delight. "I've enjoyed your company very much."

"You're too kind, Lord Gillingham," Anne urged herself to reply. After all, he was not only polite and attentive, but also a perfect gentleman. Moreover, Anne had been unable to note any of the objections Leonora had inquired after at the Barrington ball a few weeks back. All in all, there was no reason why she ought to object to his company.

But she did.

In truth, Anne had spent most of the evening trying *not* to stare at

Tobias. He had been seated not directly across from her, but a few chairs down the table on Lord Gillingham's side next to Grandmother Edie. Fortunately, that had granted her an excuse to turn her gaze in his direction as she did her best to follow Lord Gillingham's retelling of his last trip to the Continent.

Still, Tobias had been the only one on her mind. She'd stolen glimpses at him as often as inconspicuously possible. His gaze had been distant, his jaw somewhat taut as though something plagued him. Then he'd looked up, and their eyes had met for a split second before Anne had dropped her gaze in utter panic. She'd felt herself blush profusely, unable not to think of her cousin's plan in that very moment.

What would a kiss feel like?

Tobias's kiss?

"Would you care for a refreshment?" Lord Gillingham asked her in that moment, jarring Anne from her wayward thoughts. "Or perhaps a turn about the gardens?"

Anne was about to decline when she stopped. Perhaps a brisk walk through the snow would finally chase away that lingering blush that grew each time her eyes fell on her childhood friend. Indeed, it seemed whenever she lifted her gaze this night, Tobias was there, his brown eyes finding hers without fail. Was she simply imagining his presence? Or was it her cousin's blasted plan that made her overinterpret everything?

"A turn about the gardens sounds lovely," Anne told Lord Gillingham. "I must admit I feel a bit flushed."

Immediately, the young lord offered her his arm, and they strode out into the hall.

"Pardon me," someone spoke out from behind them, and Anne cringed at the sound of Louisa's voice.

Stopping, Lord Gillingham turned back to look at Louisa. "Yes? Is there something I can help you with, Lady Louisa? Perhaps you would like to join us in the gardens?"

A gentle but somewhat insincere smile came to Louisa's face. "What a lovely idea," she told Lord Gillingham with a sideways glance at Anne that made Anne want to sink into a hole in the ground. "However, I'm afraid I need to speak with my cousin about a matter of importance. Would you excuse us?"

*A matter of importance?* Anne knew that at present there was only one important matter on Louisa's mind, and she wished her cousin would simply forget about it.

Knowing Louisa, Anne was certain that hell would freeze over before that happened though.

"Of course," Lord Gillingham replied without hesitation, the look on his face one of deepest concern. "Please, if there is anything I can do."

"You're too kind," Louisa said as she slipped her arm through Anne's and pulled her back toward the drawing room, where a number of guests had collected around the pianoforte, singing Christmas carols. Joy stood in their eyes as their voices echoed through the room, adding to the warm atmosphere.

Anne, however, felt as though trapped in a block of ice.

"Where did you think you were going?" Louisa demanded under her breath.

"To get a bit of fresh air," Anne replied, trying to maintain an innocent face. "Why?"

Louisa chuckled, "As though you didn't know."

A cold shiver ran down Anne's back and her eyes widened in panic. "Now?" Her gaze swept the room, but for once Tobias was nowhere to be seen. "You said you'd wait a day or two. Why now?"

Louisa shrugged. "Why wait?" Then she all but delivered Anne into Leonora's care before hurrying off with a whispered, "You know what to do."

Tucking a strand of her dark tresses behind her ear, Leonora looked at her with compassion in her eyes. "She means well."

Anne heaved a deep sigh, wondering if Leonora would truly try to stop her if Anne made to walk off. "I know, but that doesn't mean this'll end well." Looking about herself, Anne felt her palms begin to sweat. This was a disaster waiting to happen! "What now?" she asked Leonora. "What do you...what does she have planned?"

*As though you didn't know.* Louisa's words echoed in her head.

Leonora cast her a warm smile, linking her arm with Anne's. "You are to wait here with me until the clock strikes ten."

"And then?" Anne asked, wondering why she even bothered.

Leonora hugged Anne to her. "Why are you fighting this?" she asked gently. "I saw the way you looked at him over supper. Louisa is right. You don't look at him the way she or I look at Troy. Tobias is not a brother to you, is he?"

Closing her eyes, Anne sighed, "But what if he thinks of me as a sister?" she whispered, knowing full well that not even Leonora with her sharp mind and formidable observational skills could answer that question to Anne's satisfaction.

Returning from Lord Archibald's study after a glass of brandy, Tobias and his brother were walking down the hall toward the drawing room when they spotted Lady Louisa hurrying from one of the adjoining rooms to the next. Opening a door, she peeked inside before closing it with a rather exasperated huff and then hurrying on to the next, grumbling something unintelligible under her breath.

Beside him, Phineas chuckled, "I admit I'd love to know what goes on in that devilish head of hers."

"That is no way to speak of a lady," Tobias chided his brother. Admittedly, he, too, was wondering about Lady Louisa's rather odd behavior; however, considering Phineas's poor manners, Tobias could not afford to let an opportunity to reprimand his brother slip by unused.

As expected, Phineas merely laughed, "Believe me, Brother, it was meant as a compliment."

"I doubt the lady would see it as such," Tobias protested when the lady in question spotted them.

For a second, she froze on the spot before her eyes widened, and she came charging toward them. "There you are," she exclaimed, a hint of disapproval in her voice as though they'd failed to meet her at an agreed upon time.

"It's a delight to see you again, Lulu," Phineas greeted her with a wide grin. "Are you looking for something?" The left corner of his mouth twitched. "Or rather someone?"

The implication that dripped off Phineas's voice was not lost on Lady Louisa. For a second, Tobias feared her head would explode as her eyes shot daggers and her cheeks turned a darker shade of red, steam all but coming out of her ears. "You are an utterly despicable man," she hissed, her hands balled into fists.

"You don't know the half of it," Phineas laughed, his dark gaze daring her to make good on the threat that stood in her eyes.

"Will you be quiet!" Tobias snapped at his brother before he turned to Anne's cousin. "I apologize, my lady. My brother has no manners to speak of."

Lady Louisa huffed out an annoyed breath. "That is obvious." After a final glare in his brother's direction, she seemed to put Phineas out of her mind and turned to him. "Mr. Hawke, do you have a moment? My cousin wishes to speak to you."

"Anne?" Tobias croaked as a sudden jolt went through him at the mention of her name.

Lady Louisa's face softened. "Yes, Anne. Would you come with me? I'll take you to her."

"Of course."

When Phineas fell into step beside him, Lady Louisa stopped. "Not you, *Lord Barrington*." Indeed, on her lips, it sounded like the worst sort of insult.

Of course, Phineas's response to such a challenge was laughter. "My dearest Lulu, when will you finally realize that I hold you in the highest esteem?"

Lady Louisa's brows rose as she regarded him like one would look upon an insect that had crawled onto one's dinner table. "Coming from you, that is far from a compliment." Then she spun on her heel and headed back toward the drawing room.

Phineas sighed rather wistfully as he leaned back against a marble column, his legs crossed at the ankles. "That is some woman."

Tobias shook his head at his brother and then hurried after Lady Louisa, curious what Anne wished to speak to him about.

Thus far, her time had been largely monopolized by Lord Gillingham, and Tobias had been hard pressed not to interfere in a manner that would have been considered impolite. However, he feared that he would trip over his words if he were to attempt a conversation in his current state. Had anything changed since supper? Tobias rather feared it had not.

Inhaling a deep breath, he stepped into the drawing room and spotted Anne and Lady Leonora standing near the pianoforte, a few steps away from a group of caroling guests. Both looked a bit tense. While her cousin, however, appeared no more than a tad nervous, Anne looked ready to faint. Her eyes were wide, and she was wringing her hands in a very agitated manner.

"Is something wrong?" Tobias asked, but Lady Louisa merely smiled at him.

With his eyes on Anne, Tobias watched as she took a bit of a hesitant step forward. Indeed, her whole demeanor suggested that she disagreed with whatever was happening here, and he immediately hurried to her side. "Are you all right?" he asked, running his eyes over her, trying to determine the source of her unease. "You look a bit pale."

Anne swallowed, and her lips parted as though she wished to speak. In that moment, however, Lady Louisa exclaimed, "Oh, look! They're standing under some mistletoe!"

Tobias froze as the caroling stopped and encouraging cheers went up around them. When he lifted his head, he spotted the bit of greenery dangling above their heads that Phineas had commented upon earlier that day. Indeed, he ought to have paid better attention.

His heart slammed to a halt as the implication of his situation became clear to him and a sense of dread began to crawl up his spine. Not that he'd mind kissing Anne-far from it!-but not with all these people around, staring at them.

Dimly, he wondered where his brother was. After all, Phineas would have loved to watch him squirm like this. Had he and Lady Louisa conspired to force their hand? While Tobias wouldn't put it past his brother, he rather doubted that Lady Louisa would have been able to set aside her hatred for Phineas long enough to cook up this plan. No, it had to be a coincidence.

Inhaling a deep breath, Tobias moved his gaze from the small crowd around him and looked down at Anne. Her head was slightly bowed, and she was still wringing her hands. Had she known this would happen? Had it truly been a plan to manipulate them under the mistletoe? Had Lady Louisa acted alone?

Tobias tried to swallow the lump in his throat when he realized that Anne clearly had not approved of her cousin's idea. Indeed, it seemed he finally had his answer.

Anne did not want to kiss him; that much was clear. Perhaps she truly only saw him as her friend.

When she finally lifted her gaze, Tobias felt the urge to strike something or someone for her eyes barely met his, darting left and right in a nervous fashion. "You have every right to refuse," he whispered to her, pained by the thought that she would force herself to endure his kiss.

A small smile flitted across her lips, and her eyes finally met his. "It's all right," she whispered before her gaze once more strayed from his. "Louisa would never forgive me." A breath shuddered past her lips. "You do know that this was not my idea, do you not?"

Tobias gritted his teeth, then nodded. *This couldn't possibly get any worse!*

# Chapter Seven

## AN ALMOST PERFECT PLAN

For the first time in her life, Anne was certain she was about to faint.

Bright spots danced before her eyes, and the room appeared rather unsteady, spinning in lazy circles, as she tried her best to focus her attention on the man standing in front of her.

Tobias.

Her childhood friend.

A man she'd loved all her life.

A man who suddenly managed to make her insides dance and jump and do somersaults whenever he drew near. Was that why her heart was racing as though the devil himself were after her? Was that why she couldn't seem to draw a deep breath into her lungs? Perhaps, the dizziness was of her own making. Perhaps, she simply ought to...

No, there was nothing simple. There was only Louisa's insane plan and that small little voice deep inside, urging Anne...closer.

Because, yes, she wanted this kiss.

More than she had realized.

Still, excited whispers from the guests watching them with rapt attention echoed to her ears and sent a cold shiver down Anne's back. It was, however, the look of reluctance as well as distaste on Tobias's face that made her want to run from the room. For despite her cousin's conviction as to their compatibility, *he* did not want this.

When he'd first stepped up to her, Tobias had looked confused and utterly blindsided. Then Louisa's joyous exclamation had drawn his attention to the sprig of mistletoe above their heads. Anne could still recall the way his eyes had widened. The way his jaw had tensed. She'd watched him through lowered lashes, afraid of what she might see.

And her fears had been justified.

Still, Anne had been unable to grant him a way out when he'd told her she had every right to refuse. Selfishly, she still wanted him.

Wanted this.

And so, she'd hidden behind Louisa, forcing his hand, for he would not abandon her. He would not walk away despite his own objection and shame her. After all, he was her friend.

Anne's hands were still clenched around one another, held in front of her as though to ward him off, when Tobias moved closer, bridging the small gap still between them. His gaze was unsteady, and a muscle in his jaw moved, clenching and unclenching.

Her breath caught in her throat when his right hand settled on her own, warm and comforting. Her gaze rose and met his, finding his familiar chocolate-brown eyes looking down into hers. "I'm sorry," he whispered before he lowered his head to hers.

Anne felt like the worst friend in the world for forcing him into this situation. She'd only thought of herself, her own heart, her own fears, neglecting to contemplate how Louisa's plan would affect Tobias.

*Do it fast and be done with it!* Her mind urged. *Perhaps then it won't be so bad.*

Lifting her head, Anne pinched her eyes shut and...felt the tip of her nose collide with his. His hand on hers tensed, and she could hear a soft snicker from somewhere behind him. Her eyes fluttered open a fraction, and she could see him angle his head, his lips taut. Undoubtedly, he'd heard that snicker as well.

Had there ever been a worse kiss in history?

And they hadn't even kissed yet.

Determined to see this done, Anne leaned closer. Unfortunately, Tobias seemed to have the same idea.

Once again, their noses collided before she felt his lips briefly brush the corner of her mouth.

It sent a jolt of awareness through her, but it was far from the kiss she'd been hoping for ever since Louisa had first spoken of this ludicrous idea.

Restrained laughter erupted around them as the assembled guests offered a round of applause. Both their eyes flew open, and Anne could see embarrassment darkening Tobias's face. His jaw clenched as his gaze dropped from hers in what she could only think of as resentment. Oh, what had she done?

"I'm so sorry," Anne whispered as her eyes swept the small crowd around them. Most had turned away, whispering on the quiet to one another about the worst mistletoe kiss of all times.

Only the suddenly wide-awake face of her cousins' grandmother held a measure of sympathy as she watched them from her seat near the fireplace. Oh, why couldn't at least she have slept through this disaster!

"That looked...interesting," Louisa commented with a rather contrite look on her face as she stepped up to them and pulled Anne's arm through the crook of hers. "Excuse us." She cast Tobias an apologetic smile and then pulled Anne out of the room. "What on earth was that?" her cousin whispered, a flabbergast expression upon her face when they were finally alone.

Casting uneasy glances up and down the thankfully empty corridor, Anne shrugged, then looked at her cousin. "This is what comes from all your meddling."

Louisa's eyes widened. "Don't blame this on me. I-"

"Are you all right?" Leonora asked as she came rushing down the corridor, her green eyes full of concern. "That looked awful."

Anne swallowed, "It felt awful."

"Perhaps you simply need more practice," Louisa suggested in that helpful way of hers.

Anne felt her stomach plummet. "You're not suggesting that-"

"Of course, practice makes perfect."

Shocked, mortified and furious, Anne stared at her cousin, uncertain which emotion to express first. "He didn't even *want* to kiss me," she then hissed under her breath, her finger pointing accusingly down the corridor toward the drawing room, the place of her greatest humiliation. "Did you not see his face?"

Leonora nodded, her gaze going back and forth between Anne and her sister. "He looked very tense," she confirmed. "A bit angry, too."

Anne swallowed as the magnitude of Louisa's plan washed over her. "He's my friend," she told her, "or at least he was." She drew in a deep breath. "I cannot lose him over this. I can't." She shook her head as panic washed over her. "I need to speak to him."

The thought of losing Tobias terrified Anne like no other ever had. Always had Tobias been a fixture in her life. Always had she been able to turn to him. Always had he been there. But would he after today?

Closing her eyes, Anne remembered the morning after her mother had passed away. She had been eight years old at the time, and the loss had struck her like a club wielded by a giant. Pain and grief had gripped her in an iron vice, shaking her mercilessly.

She had been Annie then, *Little Annie*, and she had not known what to do with herself, how to fill that gaping hole in her heart, how to soothe that boiling anger that made her grit her teeth until they'd ached.

Her father had been beside himself as well. He had been no help to her. Neither had her governess or Cook or Mary, the upstairs maid. No one had known what to say. All had avoided meeting her eyes.

And then Toby had found her in the stables, curled up with her kitten in the straw. He'd heard what had happened and he'd pestered his father until Lord Barrington had agreed to take him over to the Thatcher family's small estate.

And then he'd sat with her all day until the sun had gone down on Annie's first day without her mother. Toby had sat with her, his little hand on her shoulder, warm and comforting.

And he'd returned the day after that.

And the day after that.

Toby had helped her with her anger and her grief. He'd told her to yell at her mother for leaving. He'd held her when she'd succumbed to tears. He had urged her outside, made her flip pebbles across the lake and pick flowers in the meadow to place on her mother's grave. He'd thrown apples at her, forcing her to move when despair had threatened to overwhelm her. He'd pushed her in the lake and tickled her until her sides had ached. He'd told her that it was all right to be happy again.

Even without her mother.

Toby had been the one to help her through her mother's loss, the one to help her find peace again. Anne knew she could not have done it without him. She needed him. He was her friend, her best friend. She could not lose him.

Not now.

Not ever.

Blinking away the tears, Anne made to rush back to the drawing room. "I need to speak to him."

"Not now," Louisa objected, her hand closing over Anne's arm, holding her back. "You're not in your right mind now and neither is he." A hint of regret shone in her blue eyes. "You need to calm down. Come, we'll take a walk in the gardens before we retire." She looked at Leonora, who nodded in agreement. "You can speak to him tomorrow."

Allowing her cousins to pull her along, Anne sighed, "Lord Gillingham invited me to take a stroll through the gardens. If only you hadn't dragged me away." She met her cousin's gaze. "None of this would have happened."

"I'm sorry," Louisa whispered, and the look in her eyes proved that she was. "I never meant for this to go wrong."

Anne heaved a deep breath. "I know," she whispered, wishing she'd had the courage to throw herself out of the moving carriage when she'd had the chance.

~

Unable to bear the snickers a moment longer, Tobias disappeared through the side entrance, wanting nothing more but to put as much distance as possible between himself and those who'd witnessed the moment of his greatest humiliation.

Still, he couldn't fault them for whispering. If the kiss had looked as awful as it had felt, then he should consider himself fortunate that people hadn't broken down laughing so hard their sides ached and tears streamed down their faces.

Indeed, this couldn't have gone worse.

Raking his hands through his hair, Tobias spun around when he heard footsteps echoing up from behind him.

"What the hell was that?" Phin asked chuckling as he moved closer with large strides. "For it sure as hell didn't look like a kiss."

Hanging his head, Tobias let himself fall back against the wall. "You saw?"

His brother laughed, "I can't explain it," he replied with a mocking tone. "Something called to me, and I walked in the door the moment your noses collided." He laughed again. "I'm afraid to ask, but...you've done this before, haven't you?"

Heaving a deep breath, Tobias glared at his brother. "Are you only here to mock me?"

Phineas shrugged, a wide grin still on his face. "That, and to ensure you don't turn and run."

"What else would you have me do?" Tobias asked, unable to forget the tense look on Anne's face.

Leaning against the opposite wall, Phineas looked at him. "Well, as they say, if at first you don't succeed, try again." His brows rose with meaningful innuendo.

Tobias scoffed, "Are you mad? Did you not see the look of horror on her face? She didn't want this!" He shook his head in utter disbelief. "It seems reasonable to assume that it was Lady Louisa who cooked up this plan. That's why she came looking for me. That's why she used that pretext to push me under the mistletoe with Anne." He ran his hands over his face. "It was her doing, not Anne's. Anne never wanted this."

Phineas chuckled, "I admit I suspected something when she suddenly sought you out."

"Then why didn't you warn me?"

His brother shrugged. "More fun this way."

Tobias's teeth ground together in barely restrained anger. "You should leave," he hissed, pushing off the wall and proceeding farther down the corridor.

Undeterred, Phineas followed. "What makes you so certain our little Annie didn't want to kiss you?"

Tobias's feet jerked to a halt. "How can you ask that?" His eyes swept his brother's face. "I thought you saw. I even told her she was free to...refuse," again, he ran a hand over his face, remembering the slight tremor that had run through her, "but she said that her cousin would never forgive her if she did. It was Lady Louisa's plan, and Anne did not give her consent. There? Is that answer enough?"

Sighing, Phineas grasped his brother's shoulders, his dark eyes seeking his. "And did you not wonder why my dear Lulu would cook up such a plan? Why she would force the two of you to kiss?" His brows rose, his eyes watchful, waiting for an answer.

Tobias was stumped. "I..."

"Correct me if I'm wrong, dear Brother," Phin began in that rather condescending way of his, "but Anne and her cousins are fairly close, aren't they? They care for one another. Correct?" Phin's brows rose, demanding his brother acknowledge the truthfulness of his words.

Tobias nodded.

"Now, would you then consider it reasonable that my dear Lulu did what she did to spite Anne? To see her humiliated? To force her to do something she despises?"

Tobias cringed at his brother's words; still, the logic behind them gave him hope. "You think...?"

Phin nodded. "Our little Annie cares for you, and in my humble opinion, she is just as worried that you might not care for her as you are that she doesn't care for you." He rolled his eyes. "If you ask me, it's all fairly obvious. However, since you've been rather blind as of late with regard to these matters, I'll spell it out for you."

Tobias shrugged off his brother's hands. "Do you have to be such an ass?"

"Is that any way to speak to a man who's trying to help you?" Clucking his tongue, Phin shook his head.

Tobias heaved a deep sigh, willing himself to remain calm.

"Now, the only reasonable explanation for Lulu's plan is that she knows Anne cares for you, and she's just as annoyed with her inability to speak her mind as I am with yours." He fixed his brother with a pointed stare. "So, she thought what better way to end this little dance you two do around one another than to have you kiss."

Tobias frowned. "But it didn't solve anything. I still-"

"I admit Lulu's plan wasn't perfect. She-"

"Do you have to call her Lulu?" Tobias demanded, wondering about his brother's sanity. After all, despite Phineas's feigned disinterest, he seemed to care for the meddlesome Lady Louisa. Why on earth would he constantly aggravate her?

"Yes," was all his brother cared to say on the subject. "She failed to consider the strain of being observed by a bunch of obnoxious tattle-tales. If you want my advice-"

"I'm not certain I do."

Phin chuckled, "Believe me, you do." He slapped his brother on the back. "Find our little Annie alone and kiss her again. But do it right this time, or you might truly frighten her off." Grinning, he patted Tobias on the shoulder a couple of times before he turned to leave. "I'd suggest the library," he remarked over his shoulder. "Even you should be able to think of a pretext to lure her in there."

Watching his brother walk away, Tobias once more leaned against the wall at his back, his heart beating fast with this new revelation. Could it be true? Could Phineas be right? Did Anne genuinely care for him? What if he took his brother's advice, kissed her again and she...?

Tobias gritted his teeth and nodded to himself. "There's only one way to find out."

# Chapter Eight
## IN THE LIBRARY

Anne barely slept a wink all night for her mind chose to torture her by replaying the moment under the mistletoe again and again. And every time, she cringed at the sight of Tobias's taut face, the hard look in his eyes, his set jaw.

Oh, what had she done? Would he still be her friend today? How would they meet after what had happened? Was it possible to simply pretend that it never *had* happened?

As sleep proved elusive, Anne rose early. She donned a simple dress, not bothering to wake her maid, and ventured downstairs. She had no destination in mind but found herself wandering the hallways rather aimlessly. Her eyes were blind to the softly glistening snow outside as the sun began to peek over the horizon, announcing a new day. Her feet moved on their own, her gaze gliding over paintings of Lord Archibald's ancestors as well as his extensive collection of Greek urns. She heard her footfalls on the marble floors and noted their absence as she stepped across the threshold into the library. Here, a large carpet covered the floor where a sitting area had been set up near the large fireplace. Flames danced in its grate, sending out their warmth like waves rolling onto a beach.

Walking up to the window, Anne stared out into the white gardens of Windmere Park, her thoughts still lingering on what to say, how to apologize, how to right the wrong she'd done Tobias. Ought she tell him the truth about her cousin's ludicrous idea?

The thought sent a shiver down her back for Anne knew without a doubt that it would destroy her if Tobias laughed it off as she herself had pretended to more than once. For the truth was that Louisa was right. Heaven help her, but her cousin was right.

"He's no brother to me," Anne whispered into the stillness of the early morning. "Nor is he simply a friend." Still, Anne would be forever grateful if only she did not lose his friendship. A life without Tobias was one she could not even begin to imagine.

"You're up early."

At the sound of Tobias's voice, Anne spun around, her eyes wide and her cheeks burning hotter than the fire in the grate. Had he heard what she'd just foolishly said out loud?

Standing in the doorway, he looked at her, his warm gaze familiar and comforting. Although there was a hint of tension on his face, he seemed more relaxed than the day before. "Are you all right?" he asked as he stepped toward her, and for one precious moment, she found herself looking at the friend she knew.

Always had he looked out for her, his gaze watchful, easily detecting even the smallest concern that rested upon her mind. He'd always known the measurements of her heart, been a confidante to her fears and dreams. And never had she looked at him and not felt utterly at peace.

Except now. "I couldn't sleep," Anne managed to say despite the rapid beating of her traitorous heart. Why on earth did she have to do something so foolish and fall for her best friend?

"Nor I." Holding her gaze, Tobias crossed the carpet in front of the fireplace and came to stand beside her, his gaze moving to the snow-covered grounds. "I came to find you," he told her without looking at her.

Anne swallowed and turned to stand shoulder to shoulder with him, her own gaze directed out the window as well. "Why?" she dared to ask, afraid that their friendship was at a crossroads, that they would never again be able to speak openly with one another as they always had.

A muscle in his jaw twitched. "I thought we should speak." He inhaled a slow breath. "About...our kiss."

Cold panic crept up Anne's back, and she had to fight the urge to wrap her arms around herself. "What about it?" she asked through gritted teeth, forcing a bit of a chuckle into her voice. "I was hoping we could pretend it had never happened."

Tobias turned to look at her. "You did? Why?"

Too nervous to face him, Anne kept her gaze fixed on the glistening snow outside. "I admit I'm embarrassed."

Out of the corner of her eye, she could see him frown at her. "Because of the onlookers?"

"Because...because it was my first kiss." She chanced a look at him. "I suppose I...I did it wrong, judging by the snickers it-" He stepped toward her and she almost flinched, her eyes swinging around to meet his.

"You did nothing wrong," Tobias told her gently; still, a hint of anger laced his voice. "Your cousin ought not have fabricated the moment."

Anne felt her jaw drop. "You know she...?"

"I guessed as much."

"I'm so sorry," Anne stammered, feeling like a fool. Her eyes were beginning to brim with tears as she looked up at him. "Please, let us forget it ever happened."

His gaze swept over her face and his features gentled. "You said it was your first kiss." He took a step toward her and, suddenly, his fingers were tracing the line of her jaw until they gently grasped her chin, slightly tilting it upward.

Anne almost dropped to the ground with shock at the soft touch, at his nearness, at...the look in his eyes. "What are you doing?" she whispered breathlessly. "Why...why are you looking at me like that?"

A slow smile teased the corners of his mouth upward before his eyes dropped from hers. She could all but feel his gaze trace the line of her lips and her heart stumbled in her chest. Her knees grew weak, and she had to draw in a deep breath to focus her thoughts.

"Do you object?" Tobias asked, his meaning unmistakably clear as he moved closer still.

Anne knew not what to think...or do...or say. "But...I...We...we've tried and...and it was a disaster. Why-?"

A surprised chuckle rumbled in his throat, "A disaster? That's a bit harsh, wouldn't you say?"

Anne frowned as a bit of the old ease that had always existed between them re-emerged. Her lips curled into a smile. "What would *you* call it then?"

Closing his eyes briefly, Tobias laughed. "Very well. It was a disaster."

"Precisely." Bolstered by the sense of normalcy that washed over her, Anne stood a bit taller. Still, Tobias's fingers continued to linger on her chin, and her skin tingled with the touch. "Then why try again?" she demanded boldly. "There's nothing to be gained." Deep down, a little voice screamed at her to shut up and accept what he was offering. Because what he was offering was a kiss, wasn't it?

A kiss to make up for the one that had so horribly gone wrong. A kiss without onlookers. A kiss on their own terms. A kiss Anne wanted with all her heart.

"I disagree," he replied, his gaze now serious as his fingers on her chin tightened. "Close your eyes."

A weak breath shuddered past Anne's lips. "Are you serious?"

"Close your eyes," he demanded, not allowing her to distract him.

"But...?"

A small smile teased his lips, and he shook his head ever so slightly. "Close...your...eyes."

Terrified, and yet, utterly tempted, Anne finally did as he bid her. Her eyelids fluttered closed, and to her great dismay, the memory of their noses colliding instantly resurfaced.

Only this time was different.

This time, Anne felt him lean closer, the warmth of his body reaching out to her like the fire in the grate. She felt his breath brush gently over her skin, tickling her lips, parting them as a small gasp escaped her. Her lids began to flutter, urging her to peek, to see that he was truly there, that she had not strayed into a dream.

"Don't you dare," he growled against her lips, a hint of humor in his voice.

"I cannot bear the suspense any l-"

His mouth claimed hers swiftly, and despite everything that had led up to this moment, it was thoroughly unexpected.

Her heart and mind were reeling from the sensations that rushed through her body. Everything felt foreign, new, utterly unfamiliar, but so very right. The gentle pressure of his lips, the soft grasp of his fingers upon her chin, the way his other hand brushed down her arm and then settled upon her waist.

Pushing closer, Anne responded to his kiss on instinct alone, wondering how she suddenly knew what to do. Nothing felt awkward as it had before, and her hands snaked up his chest, her fingertips coming to rest against the side of his neck. His pulse beat as fast as her own, and she wondered if he too felt unhinged and at peace at the same time.

Unlike their mistletoe kiss from the day before, this kiss was everything Anne had dreamed of and more and she sank into Tobias's arms on a contented sigh.

# Chapter Nine

## THE COMPETITOR INTERVENES

Resisting the urge to deepen their kiss, Tobias held her close, overcome by the strength of this sudden need for her. He'd loved Anne all his life, and yet, this felt different.

Her lips were soft and curious under his own, and her skin felt velvety and warm to his touch. Her heart beat fast as she leaned into him, welcoming his kiss, his touch...

...welcoming him.

*Our little Annie cares for you*, his brother's voice echoed in his mind and, in that moment, Tobias wanted nothing more than to believe it. To know that it was true. Was there more between them than friendship? Could Anne truly love him? Not like a brother, but-

Footsteps echoed up the hallway outside the library, drawing closer to the door Tobias had foolishly left ajar.

Anne had to have heard it as well for she stilled, then broke their kiss, her blue eyes wide. "Did you hear that?" she whispered before her gaze darted past his shoulder.

Grabbing her hand, Tobias pulled her behind the tall bookshelf, separating the sitting area from the main part of the library. "Quiet," he whispered as they hid behind tall volumes filled with archeological expertise.

Staring into each other's eyes, they heard the door swing open quietly before soft footsteps proceeded into the room. "Miss Thatcher, are you in here?" came Lord Gillingham's voice, and Tobias felt a worrisome urge to pound the man into the ground well up in his chest.

Anne's hands tensed on his, and a warning look came to her wide eyes before she shook her head at him.

Tobias gritted his teeth, wondering if she simply knew him too well or if his murderous thoughts were written all over his face.

Peeking above the rim of two particularly thick volumes, Anne frowned, then drew in a deep breath and met his eyes. She pointed at his chest and then at the ground, urging him to stay where he was.

Tobias raised his brows, asking what she planned to do.

With two fingers, she imitated someone walking in the direction of the door, namely herself.

Tobias gritted his teeth against the objections that rose in his heart. Still, she was right. They couldn't be found together. It would compromise her, and even though their second kiss had been life-altering for him, Tobias could not be certain how Anne felt about it. And he would never force her hand.

Nodding, he took a step back and allowed her to pass, returning the smile she cast at him over her shoulder as best as he could. Then he watched her take a deep breath and step around the tall shelf. "Lord Gillingham, is that you?"

A large smile came to the man's face, and Tobias's hands balled into fists. "Good morning, Miss Thatcher," Lord Gillingham greeted her with a bow. "I'd hoped to find you here after your cousin told me that you'd risen early. I remembered you mentioning your fondness for the written word and decided to try my luck." He offered her his arm. "It would seem Fortune smiles on me. May I escort you down to breakfast?"

Smiling at the man, Anne slipped her hand through the crook of Lord Gillingham's arm. "Yes, thank you. I admit I'm rather famished."

A few steps brought them to the doorway where Lord Gillingham paused. "Did you choose a book you wished to read?" His gaze returned to the tall-standing shelves. "I apologize if I interrupted you."

"I couldn't decide," Anne told him. "I'll come back later." Then she made to step across the threshold but stopped when Lord Gillingham failed to move.

Tobias frowned as the man smiled at Anne in a rather odd way, then pointed upward. "It would seem we find ourselves under some mistletoe, my dear Miss Thatcher."

Tobias's heart almost beat out of his chest as he stared at Anne. She had stilled at Lord Gillingham's words and was now slowly raising her gaze. When her eyes fell on the small branch, she drew in a slow breath. Her jaw tensed, and he thought to see a hint of reluctance come to her face.

Lord Gillingham chuckled, "I've heard of yesterday's unfortunate encounter." The man's gaze sought Anne's. "Perhaps you'll have better luck with me."

Red hot jealousy burnt in Tobias's veins, and he could barely keep himself from charging out of his hiding spot. If he'd still needed an answer as to how he felt about Anne, it now seemed perfectly clear. Still, he could not allow her to be compromised, which was exactly what would happen if Lord Gillingham learned that Anne had not been alone in the library.

Nevertheless, the thought of another man kissing *his* Anne turned Tobias's stomach. It was wrong.

Simply wrong.

She was his, was she not?

At least, he wanted her to be. But what was he to do now?

"Lord Gillingham, perhaps...," Anne began as the young lord stepped closer, intent on claiming his prize. Her eyes flitted over her shoulder, and for the barest of seconds, they met Tobias's before she lifted a hand to stop Lord Gillingham's approach. "I do not believe it wise to-"

The man's hand grasped Anne's, pulling her toward him. "I admit I've been hoping for such an opportunity."

"My lord, I-"

"There you are!" exclaimed a familiar voice a moment before Lady Louisa appeared in the door frame. "We've been looking all over for you."

Lady Louisa's gaze moved from Anne to Lord Gillingham and then, with no more than a glance, she took note of the mistletoe above their heads. Instantly, her jaw set, and her eyes met Anne's. "You must excuse us once more, Lord Gillingham," she said with an utterly sweet smile. "But I require my cousin's aid in a most serious matter yet again."

Lord Gillingham sighed, clearly displeased with Lady Louisa's interference. Tobias, on the other hand, breathed a sigh of relief. Never in his life had he been this grateful for Lady Louisa's meddlesome tendencies.

Indeed, it was good to know she was on his side.

After Anne and her cousin had walked away, Lord Gillingham's footfalls also retreated, and silence once more fell over the library. Running a hand over his face, Tobias stepped out of his hiding place, his gaze gliding over the peaceful gardens, slumbering under a white blanket.

He'd kissed her; and she'd kissed him back. The thought brought a smile to his lips, and Tobias hardly knew how to contain the joy that surged through his heart.

"I see you took my advice."

At the sound of his brother's voice, Tobias closed his eyes. "Why is it that you always appear when it's least convenient?"

Phineas chuckled as his feet carried him to his brother's side. "It is my special talent, I would say." Leaning casually against the wall, Phin looked at him, the look in his eyes one of inquisitive watchfulness. "I assume you were successful." His brows rose in meaningful innuendo.

Tobias exhaled a deep breath and turned to look at his brother. "And why would you assume that?"

"Because you look like the cat who got the cream, that's why," Phineas replied with another chuckle. "Will you now finally admit that you love our little Annie?"

Unable not to, Tobias smiled. "There's no point in denying it now, is there?"

Phineas shook his head. "Very little. But then, you've always been a bad liar."

"I'll take that as a compliment."

His brother shrugged. "I suppose that depends on your perspective." He pushed off the wall and came to stand in front of Tobias. "So, when will you ask her?"

Tobias frowned. "Ask her?"

"To marry you!" Phineas rolled his eyes. "Please, don't tell me I'll need to talk you into this as well."

Tobias turned to leave. "I'll not discuss this with you, dear Brother." After all, who knew what Phineas would do with the information obtained? First, Tobias needed to speak to Anne-alone!-and find out where her heart was.

If it beat for him...or not.

If she'd merely been taken with her first-or second-kiss...or if she felt that awareness between them as well.

Tobias could only hope that she did, for he could not bear the thought of losing her to another.

At least, it seemed that Lord Gillingham did not hold her favor. That was encouraging!

# Chapter Ten

## A BLIND FOOL…

Louisa's hand felt like an iron vice around her arm as she dragged Anne back down the corridor toward their chambers. Just as she pushed open the door, Leonora came rushing around the opposite corner. Upon spotting them, her eyes widened, and she quickened her step, hastening to their side. "Oh, you found her!" Her gaze moved to Anne. "Are you all right? We were quite worried when we found you gone this morning."

Shooing them all into her chamber, Louisa then closed the door. "I found her with Gillingham under some mistletoe," she snapped, open disapproval in her voice. "I knew that man was up to something."

Leonora's jaw dropped. "Did he kiss you?"

"I-" Anne began; however, she didn't get any further.

"I do believe I got there just in time," Louisa rushed to say, and her blue eyes swiveled to Anne. "Didn't I?"

Anne nodded. "You did. Thank you." A grateful smile came to her lips, for after kissing Tobias, the last thing she would have wanted to do had been to share a mistletoe kiss with Lord Gillingham.

Louisa patted Anne's shoulder reassuringly before she began to pace the length of the room, her eyes moving fast as words poured from her mouth. "What happened proves that you were right about

Lord Gillingham. He clearly has *certain* intentions toward you." Her gaze rose to meet Anne's. "And that means that you'll need to make up your mind about our dear Mr. Hawke."

The mere mention of Tobias brought a flutter to Anne's stomach, and she couldn't help a deep smile from spreading over her face.

Instantly, Louisa's eyes narrowed. "What happened?" she asked, hopeful suspicion in her voice that made Leonora turn and look at Anne with renewed interest.

Anne sighed contentedly. "He kissed me."

"Lord Gillingham?" Leonora asked, her eyes going wide. "But I thought you said-"

"Not him!" Louisa interrupted with a wide grin. "She's talking about our dear Mr. Hawke."

Leonora clasped her hands together. "He kissed you? How? Why? When? Where?"

Anne nodded, loving her cousins for their excitement.

Louisa put a finger to her lips. "I'd say, when and where are easy: a few minutes ago, in the library, am I not right?" Biting her lower lip, Anne nodded. "How? Well, judging from the look on your face, I think it's safe to assume that this kiss went significantly better than the last." Anne felt her face turn as red as a tomato. "Then, there is the question of why?" Louisa took a step toward Anne. "Why did he kiss you?"

Needing a bit of space, Anne ventured over to the window and looked down at the frozen grounds. "He found me in the library, and I apologized for our kiss. I told him that...it had been my first and-"

"Your first?" Louisa exclaimed, and as Anne turned to look at her over her shoulder, she found her cousin's eyes as round as plates. "Well, that certainly explains yesterday's disaster."

A weak breath shuddered past Anne's lips as the word reminded her of the moment she'd shared with Tobias only moments ago. Still, she could not deny that there was a bit of a dark cloud hanging over that precious moment. Why had Tobias kissed her? Why indeed?

Sighing, Anne turned to look at her cousins. "I don't know why he kissed me. I was so nervous, but then suddenly, it felt like...us again." Her gaze moved from Louisa to Leonora. "Do you think he only kissed me to make amends for that awkward mistletoe kiss? Because he knew that it had been my first? Did he feel guilty? Did he pity me?" The thought made her insides twist and turn.

Louisa chuckled, "You know I love you, do you not?" she asked as she stepped forward and grasped Anne's hands.

Anne nodded.

"Therefore, saying this hurts me more than it hurts you, but it must be said." Louisa inhaled a bit of an overly dramatic breath and then met Anne's gaze head-on. "You're a fool."

Anne stilled. "Pardon me?"

"Well, it's either that or you're blind." She lifted a hand and held it up to Anne's face. "How many fingers am I holding up?"

Anne frowned, staring at Louisa's hand before moving her gaze to her cousin's face. "What on earth are you talking about?"

Louisa shrugged. "Well, you must be as blind as a bat if you cannot see that that man loves you."

Anne's jaw dropped, and her heart stumbled.

"You cannot know that," Leonora threw in as she stepped forward, giving up her observational post for a more active one. "Although I do hope you're right, we cannot know if Mr. Hawke did not kiss Anne for any of the reasons she listed."

"Oh, he didn't!" Louisa objected vehemently.

Leonora crossed her arms over her chest. "How would you know?"

"I simply do," Louisa insisted. "I was right before, wasn't I?" She looked from Leonora to Anne, a challenge in her wide blue eyes. When neither one of them objected, she turned to Anne. "You do not see him as a brother, do you?"

Smiling, Anne shook her head. Indeed, here and now, that thought seemed ludicrous. How could she ever have thought of him as a brother?

"Then trust me now," Louisa pleaded as she once again grasped Anne's hands. "Go claim that man before Lord Gillingham manages to spoil everything."

Anne swallowed, now more terrified than ever before to have been mistaken. To lose Tobias despite her cousin's reassurances. No longer would she be satisfied with his friendship. No, now, she wanted more. A curse of her own making. But did he as well?

"I promise I'll speak to him," Anne mumbled, at a loss as to how to breach such a sensitive subject. "Perhaps tomorrow or-"

Louisa groaned, "At your pace, I'll die of old age before you two finally tie the knot!"

Anne stared at her cousin. "How can you be so certain?"

"I simply am," Louisa told her with a gentle smile. "If you were me and you'd seen what I've seen, you would be as well. Trust me, dear cousin, and don't wait too long. Or you'll forever regret it."

# Chapter Eleven

## LADY LOUISA'S MOMENT

With two dozen guests staying at Windmere Park, breakfast was a rather loud affair. Cheerful voices echoed up and down the table as plans were discussed, discarded, altered and ultimately agreed upon. Tobias, however, only had eyes for Anne.

Never in his life had he been as oblivious to the world around him as he was now. He barely noticed what he put in his mouth and chewed for his focus lay with the bewitching, young lady two seats down on the opposite side of the table.

So close.

But still, too far away.

Fortunately, this morning, she was flanked by her two cousins. They whispered to each other confidently, and occasionally their eyes looked across the table at him. While her cousins' eyes swept over him with a somewhat less restrained directness, Anne only ever glanced in his direction, quickly dropping her gaze back to her plate the moment their eyes met.

Tobias smiled at the somersault his heart did whenever that happened, and he could not wait to speak to her again.

Perhaps even kiss her again.

Would she want him to?

If only he knew.

After breakfast, many headed outside to the frozen lake. The sun shone brightly, and the air was brisk and refreshing. Snow had stopped falling overnight, but now lay in thick layers upon the ground. Footmen had cleared it off the frozen lake, though, and people were gathering on its banks, strapping on skates.

"I assume you have yet to speak to her," Phineas remarked as he came to sit next to Tobias on one of the benches that had been set around the small lake, "for she is over there and you are here." His brows rose, demanding an answer.

"I fail to see how this is any of your business," Tobias replied defensively as he strapped on his own skates. "I will speak to her when the time is right."

Phineas scoffed, "Then you'll be waiting forever, dear Brother, for I have no doubt you'll always manage to conjure a reason to delay." His hand settled upon Tobias's shoulder. "Speak to her. Now." His other hand gestured across the lake to where Anne and Leonora were skating near an overhanging willow tree. "Before it's too late."

Tobias tensed the moment he caught sight of Lord Gillingham. The man's gaze was fixed on Anne as he skated closer, the intent in his eyes unmistakable.

Phineas chuckled, "I wonder whose idea it was to hang one of those kissing boughs upon the tree there." He laughed, his eyes moving to settle upon Tobias. "Lord Archibald seems oddly dedicated to uphold this charming tradition."

Swallowing hard, Tobias noted that his brother was right. Not far from where Anne was skating, a bright green mistletoe sprig dangled from the tree above. "Bloody hell!" Tobias cursed when Lord Gillingham reached the cousins' side, greeting first Leonora and then Anne.

The man offered her his arm, and she reluctantly accepted it, unaware that he was urging her closer to the kissing bough.

Tobias would have jumped to his feet had he not been wearing skates. As it was, all he could do was surge upward, his gaze fixed upon his greatest fear when his brother's tense voice cut through his thoughts. "What the hell is *she* doing?"

Looking up, Tobias found Phineas staring at Lady Louisa who came skating over from the other side of the lake with lightning speed. Her gaze was locked on Anne, and she didn't appear to have any intent of slowing down.

Meanwhile, it seemed Anne had finally realized Lord Gillingham's intention for her face flushed red and she seemed to be looking about herself as though searching for a way out.

Tobias's heart warmed at the thought that once again she did not wish to kiss the persistent lord. Still, sometimes persistence won out!

Not today, though.

Everything happened in a blur.

One moment, Anne felt her stomach drop at the sight of Lord Gillingham drawing closer for a kiss-for the second time that day no less!-and in the next, Louisa crashed into her, knocking her down onto the frozen lake. The air rushed from her lungs, and her right hip throbbed a bit where it connected with the ice.

Louisa ended up sprawled on top of her, her blond curls tickling Anne's nose. "Oh, I'm so sorry, dearest," her cousin exclaimed, deepest concern in her voice as she made to scramble back onto her feet. "I tried to stop but…" Her voice trailed off, an apologetic look in her eyes.

"I'm fine," Anne assured her as Lord Gillingham helped her to her feet.

"Are you sure?" Leonora asked as her eyes swept over Anne, no doubt looking for injuries. "That looked awful."

"She truly ought to lie down," Lord Gillingham insisted, rather unwilling to relinquish his hold on Anne's arm. "I'll have Lord Archibald send for the doctor."

"I'm fine," Anne insisted with equal vehemence, starting to become vexed when the man refused to release her arm. "Do you mind?" she asked with a pointed stare. "I'm quite capable of walking on my own. I've been doing it for almost twenty years."

Louisa chuckled, and when Anne turned to look at her cousin, she thought to see something there that made her pause. "I quite agree, Lord Gillingham," Louisa said with a serious face; still, Anne could not help but notice the slight quirk in her cousin's lips. "Leonora, would you help her back to her room and see to her?"

Nodding, Leonora took Anne's other arm and pulled her toward the bank and the bench situated not far off. "Come. We'll head inside. You could use something warm to drink."

Anne glanced back over her shoulder and noticed not only a fallen expression on Lord Gillingham's face, but also a rather triumphant one on Louisa's. "This was no accident," Anne mumbled before she turned to look at Leonora. "She crashed into me on purpose."

Leonora paused and looked back at Lord Gillingham. "Would you rather she hadn't?"

Anne drew in a deep breath, and her gaze moved to the other side of the frozen lake where Tobias stood. His posture seemed tense even from a distance, and Anne allowed herself to believe that he too was grateful for Louisa's interference. "She did it to protect me from Lord Gillingham," Anne whispered to herself.

Beside her, Leonora nodded. "She can be quite troublesome at times, but she's also a fierce ally to have." Love and admiration swung in Leonora's voice, and when Anne turned to look at her cousin, she found a warm smile on her face.

Anne sighed, "I always wanted a sister."

"Careful what you wish for," Leonora chuckled as they sat down on the bench to remove the skates from their boots. "Gratitude can be quickly replaced by annoyance."

Anne laughed, believing every word. Still, she would thank her cousin for her interference. After all, Tobias was the only man Anne wanted to kiss.

That, at least, she was certain of now.

# Chapter Twelve

## ...OR TWO

Relieved, Tobias watched Anne and her cousin, Lady Leonora, return to the house, leaving behind a somewhat desolate-looking Lord Gillingham.

"That was close," Phineas remarked beside him. "I hope you'll heed my advice now and not delay any further."

Tobias sighed and nodded, "I should speak to her."

"Indeed, you should," said a slightly annoyed voice to his right.

When he turned, Tobias found Lady Louisa standing on the bank, her arms akimbo and a bit of a frustrated glare in her blue eyes. Without him noticing, she had made her way across the frozen lake, then removed her skates and was now watching him with great displeasure.

Intrigued, Phineas approached her, his dark gaze raking over her in open admiration. "You're quite a menace, my dear Lulu."

Her jaw tensed as she looked past him, ignoring Phineas as best as she could. "I know you care for her," Lady Louisa said to Tobias without preamble, her eyes watchful, no doubt noting the way he all but sighed at the mere mention of Anne. "Why then do you stand idly by and allow another to steal kisses?"

Tobias tensed. "What ought I have done? I was too far away."

Lady Louisa's lips curled into a wicked smile. "Not this morning in the library." Her brows rose in challenge. "I interfered and prevented the worst as I did again just now. However, I won't be able to keep Lord Gillingham away from her indefinitely." She took a step toward him, but then flinched, sucking in a sharp breath. "You need-"

"Are you hurt?" The easy smile slid off Phineas's face as he grasped her hand, his gaze falling to her right foot.

"I'm fine," Lady Louisa snapped, jerking her hand out of his. "I'd appreciate it if you didn't touch me, *Lord Barrington*." Her voice was icy, and Tobias did not fail to notice that it seemed to cut his brother as few things ever had before.

"Why?" Tobias asked. "Not that I'm not grateful for your interference, but why?"

Lady Louisa sighed, a rather indulgent look coming to her eyes. "Because I want to see her happy and because I believe you're the one to achieve it." Her gaze warmed. "She loves you, and I feel deeply confident in my conclusion that you love her as well. Is that not so?"

Staring at Lady Louisa, Tobias barely heard the remainder of her words as her first three continued to echo in his mind. *She loves you.*

Lady Louisa exhaled an exasperated sigh, "Apparently, you're as blind as she is." She took another step closer, cringing once again as she put weight on her right foot. "How can you not see it?" She shook her head in disbelief. "Be that as it may, if you no longer think of her as *Little Annie*, then you need to act. Fast."

Phineas scoffed, "That's precisely what I said."

Shock came to Lady Louisa's face as she turned to look upon him for the first time. "You did?" Her lips thinned in something resembling disgust.

In answer, Phineas wiggled his brows in that deeply annoying way. "Believe me, it came as quite a shock to me as well that we actually agree on something. A grave sign, indeed, for it surely prophesies the end of the world as we know it." Then he laughed.

Rolling her eyes, Lady Louisa returned to ignoring Phineas, which was generally sound advice. Again, she took a painful step toward Tobias. "Well? What do you intend to do?"

"You should have a doctor look at your ankle," Tobias advised, equally determined not to discuss his plans with Lady Louisa. The woman was as intrusive as Phineas. Why the two of them didn't get along was beyond him.

"Don't try to distract me," Lady Louisa hissed, annoyance darkening her face. "You-"

"I'm not trying to distract you," Tobias insisted. "However, I do believe you're in significant pain. You should-"

"He's right," Phineas exclaimed, and without another word, he swept Lady Louisa into his arms and marched back toward the house.

Tobias couldn't help but laugh as the lady protested not only loudly, but also with severe-looking smacks to his brother's upper body-anything within reach! Phineas, however, seemed to find her reaction deeply amusing as his hold on her never wavered.

Perhaps Anne was right. Perhaps those two would either kill each other before the year was out or fall madly in love.

Tobias sighed, "Anne," he whispered to himself, loving the sound of her name for it conjured her beautiful face. "Will you marry me?" he mumbled, imagining what it would be like to have her by his side for all the days to come.

Would she say *yes*?

"Truly, Leo, I'm fine," Anne told her cousin after they'd returned to her chamber. "I'll probably have a bit of a bruise on my hip, but other than that I suffered no injury."

"I'm glad," Leonora replied, both of her hands wrapped around a warm cup of tea as they sat in Anne's chamber, trying to warm up. "I admit it looked quite horrifying the way she crashed into you."

"That's Louisa for you," Anne remarked with a smile. "She never does anything half-heartedly."

Leonora grinned. "No, she doesn't. Sometimes that worries me for I fear that-"

"You foul-mouthed oaf! Put me down this instant!"

Both cousins froze, their eyes widening as they heard Louisa's booming voice echo through the closed door to Anne's chamber.

"What is going on?" Anne asked as she hurried to cross to the door, then pulled it open.

"Miss Thatcher, Lady Leonora," Phineas greeted them with a smirk on his face as he walked by, a struggling Louisa in his arms. Ignoring her protests, he carried her a few steps farther, then pushed open the door to her chamber and walked inside.

"What happened?" Leonora asked, her eyes wide with concern as both cousins hurried after them.

"He won't put me down!" Louisa snapped, once more shoving against Phineas's chest. "This poor excuse for a man won't-"

"She twisted her foot with that little stunt of hers," Phineas explained over his shoulder. "I asked to send for a doctor, but I suggest you cool her ankle until he arrives."

Leonora nodded and immediately darted off.

"Put me down!" Louisa hissed yet again as Phineas moved to settle her upon the bed. However, another one of her abrupt shoves against his chest promptly made him lose his balance.

Anne stared as Phineas with Louisa in his arms tipped forward and they both fell onto the bed. Phineas barely managed to catch himself with one outstretched arm, their faces now close enough for a kiss. "If you wanted me in your bed," Phineas whispered with a grin, "all you had to do was ask."

Anne bit her lip to keep a grin from showing on her face for the look in Louisa's eyes spoke only remotely of annoyance. Indeed, there was something there that whispered of temptation and desire held in check. Perhaps Anne was not the only one hesitant to admit where her heart truly lay.

"Get off me!" Louisa hissed, once she'd recovered her wits. "Or I swear I will end you!"

Chuckling, Phineas rose to his feet, "Charming as always, dear Lulu." His gaze moved to her ankle, and the expression on his face sobered. "For once, take care of yourself." Then he turned, smiled at Anne and walked out the door...

...right past a very curious looking Grandma Edie.

Pushing herself up into a seated position, Louisa glared at the door. "That man is despicable! He had the nerve to-"

"To carry you to your chamber all the way from the lake," Anne interrupted as she came to sit beside her cousin. "Is that not so?"

Closing the door, Grandma Edie settled into an armchair in the corner, her pale eyes watchful. "He carried you inside?" she chuckled with a glance at the door through which Phineas had left. "Perhaps he discovered some manners after all."

"I didn't ask him to!" Louisa snapped defensively. "Quite on the contrary, he refused to set me down!"

"But it was kind of him to do so," Anne insisted, sharing a bit of a complicit look with Louisa's grandmother. "To carry you back to your chamber." She marveled as she glimpsed a moment of contemplation flit over Louisa's face. However, it passed before it could linger.

"Who knows why?" her cousin hissed. "I have no doubt he'll mock me about it endlessly." Her teeth ground together before she finally managed to shake off the thoughts that riled her. "Let's forget about that odious man and talk about our dear Mr. Hawke."

Anne inhaled a deep sigh, "I promised I would speak to him and I shall."

Leaning back against her pillows, Louisa reached for Anne's hand. "He loves you. He all but admitted as much."

Anne tensed as a sense of foreboding washed over her. "What did you do, Louisa? Please tell me you didn't..." She couldn't bring herself to say the words, but her head moved from side to side as though the movement could undo what Louisa had so foolishly done.

Louisa patted Anne's hand. "I'm sorry, dearest, but it slipped out." She sighed, "Truly it had to be said."

Anne stared at her cousin. "You told him I loved him?" she asked in horror.

Grandma Edie chuckled. "Well played, my girl."

Louisa cast her grandmother a warm smile before her gaze returned to Anne. "Why don't you want him to know?"

"Because...because..." Lost for words, Anne knew not what to think, let alone say.

"I can see that you're afraid," Louisa replied, her hands settling on the mattress before she pushed herself back against the pillows into a more erect position, "and I understand why you would be. But if you allow that fear to hold you back, you'll spend the rest of your days dreaming of a life with Tobias instead of living it. Is that what you want?"

Anne closed her eyes. "But what if he doesn't love me?"

"He does," Louisa insisted.

"He does," Grandma Edie agreed as she settled deeper into the armchair, her head coming to rest against the upholstery.

"How do you know?" Anne demanded, looking from one to the other.

Exhaling another exasperated breath, Louisa grasped Anne's hands anew, a rather impatient insistence in her grip. "Have I not been right about this from the start? Why are you so afraid to trust me? To trust yourself?" Her blue eyes looked deep into Anne's. "When he kissed you, what did it feel like?"

A smile teased Anne's lips. However, she could not help but feel a bit uneasy discussing this with her cousin's grandmother seated only a few steps away. Fortunately, a rather uneasy glance in Grandma Edie's direction confirmed that the dowager had once again dozed off as she often did quite unexpectedly.

"See?" Louisa declared triumphantly, interpreting Anne's smile for what it was. "Now, would you stop worrying and go and speak to him? You're giving me a headache!" Sighing, she rubbed her temples.

A part of Anne wanted nothing more but to seek out Tobias and see Louisa's words confirmed. Another part, however, still would not let go of the *what ifs*, fearing she could not gain anything from revealing her feelings, but would instead lose the best friend she'd ever had. "You had no right to tell him," Anne squeaked, well-aware that she was merely stalling for time. Her hands were trembling, and she feared her heart would beat out of her chest at the thought of facing Tobias.

Louisa, of course, saw right through her. "Stop trying to distract me," her cousin snapped gently. "What is done is done. Now, stop hiding and go speak to him." She waved her hands, shooing Anne off the bed. "And avoid Lord Gillingham for I won't be there to save you another time." Her brows rose, and she gestured to her ankle.

Anne smiled at her. "Thank you...for saving me."

"What is family for?" Louisa replied with a devilish grin. "I admit it was fun!"

"But your ankle," Anne insisted. "You-"

"Out!" Louisa snapped, a warning glare in her eyes. "Now!" Her right arm snapped outward, and her forefinger pointed at the door. "I mean it! Go!"

Inhaling a deep breath, Anne complied, hoping despite her jittery nerves that this day would end as promising as it had begun.

With another kiss!

From the right man, of course.

# Chapter Thirteen
## OUT INTO THE SNOW

Pulling on a dry pair of boots as well as her heavy winter cloak, Anne headed back outside.

The cold air felt wonderful upon her heated cheeks as her eyes swept the grounds, looking for Tobias. Many guests were still ice-skating while others had begun a snowball fight near the maze in the western half of the garden. The tall hedges provided a good shield behind which one could duck when another missile came flying at one's head. Laughter echoed across the glistening snow, reminding Anne of the joyful winter days she'd shared with Tobias and Phin when they had been children. Was there any chance they could hold on to this bond now that they were grown?

"Are you looking for someone?"

Looking over her shoulder, Anne found Phineas standing only a few feet away. "I might be," she replied as a nervous shiver snaked down her back. It would have been easy enough to blame it on the cold; however, Anne knew that she could no longer hide from the truth.

Louisa would never let her.

Phineas grinned. "Am I right to assume that you're looking for my brother?" He moved closer, his dark gaze watchful and...knowing.

Oh, so knowing.

Anne swallowed. "Perhaps."

Phin laughed, and his large hands settled upon her shoulders as his eyes looked into hers. "You're as bad as he is, dear Annie," he said gently, humor teasing his voice. "I'll go and fetch him for you, but you have to promise me that you won't let him get away."

Anne inhaled a shuddering breath. If only it were that easy! After all, Tobias did have a say in what would come of...of their kiss, of that deep, unsettling, all-consuming feeling that made her heart race and her breath lodge in her throat. It was not merely her decision, but his as well.

"Promise me!" Phin insisted.

Anne nodded, unable to utter a single word.

Phineas grinned, giving her shoulders a slight squeeze before he walked away in the direction of the lake, a soft chuckle echoing after him.

Anne inhaled a deep breath, rubbing her hands together against the cold. Her thoughts were racing as much as her heart, trying to conjure the right words to say. Never had she been good at expressing what lived in her heart. Somehow it had always simply been a known truth between her and Tobias. They'd been friends, almost family. She'd always loved him, and he'd always loved her. They'd never said it, never spoken about it, and yet, they'd known.

They'd simply known.

How on earth was she to tell him what lived in her heart now? Was she simply to blurt it out?

Her feet carried her around in little circles, her gaze drawn to the other guests still engaged in a snowball fight, laughing, their faces flushed with excitement. Oh, if only she could join in and ignore the nagging fear that lingered in her chest!

"Miss Thatcher, what a surprise to see you!"

Anne almost groaned at the sound of Lord Gillingham's voice behind her. Her eyes closed, and she inhaled a calming breath before turning to face him.

"I'd thought you'd remain indoors after your ordeal," he remarked as long strides carried him closer. "Are you well?" His gaze swept over her.

Anne felt a shiver run down her spine; and this shiver was not of the teasing, tingling kind; the kind that stole one's breath and quickened one's heart. No, this shiver spoke of reluctance and unease. "I am well," Anne told him, annoyed that he'd found her again. "As I've said before. Is there a reason you don't seem to believe me?"

A hint of surprise came to his face at her harshly spoken words. "Not at all. I'm merely worried."

Anne sighed, "I appreciate your concern; however, it is not necessary."

"Would you like to take a stroll around the gardens?" Lord Gillingham asked, stepping closer and offering her his arm.

Anne glanced over her shoulder. "I'm afraid I cannot. I'm waiting for a friend."

Lord Gillingham's smile faded. "It seems we're always interrupted." He moved closer, and his gaze sought hers in a way that made Anne want to turn and run. "I lost not one, but two chances to kiss you today." His gaze drifted lower to touch upon her lips. "But perhaps a third will present itself."

Repelled by his frank words, Anne took a step back. "You've been very kind, my lord," she told him, doing her best not to sound as repulsed as she felt, "but I feel compelled to inform you that...my heart beats for another." There, she'd said it! Not to Tobias, but at least she'd managed to tell Lord Gillingham how she felt.

Thus far, Anne had been reluctant, hoping that the man would come to understand her short, indifferent answers and lack of interest for what they were. She'd hoped he would realize that she did not care for him and bestow his attentions elsewhere. However, it would seem open words were needed after all.

Lord Gillingham's face darkened. "That cannot be true."

"But it is," Anne insisted, wishing he would simply take his leave and go. "My heart beats for another and has for a while."

His lips thinned. "You've misled me," he gritted out on a hissed breath.

Anne frowned. "I've done no such thing. I've spoken to you as a friend, no more and no less. But I am sorry if you've misunderstood my intentions."

The look in his eyes remained hard and, instead of taking a step back, Lord Gillingham took one closer. "You-"

"I must insist you leave!" Anne objected to his inappropriate approach. No longer concerned for his feelings, she drew back her shoulders and lifted her chin. "Now!"

Lord Gillingham tensed, but he kept his distance. Still, he seemed more than a bit reluctant to comply, no doubt another accusation on the tip of his tongue. However, before he could give it voice, a snowball hit him hard on the side of his face, sending him sprawling into the snow.

"She's looking for you."

Lost in thought, Tobias flinched at the sound of his brother's voice. "Pardon me?" He turned to look at Phineas and found him cutting his way in-between the leafless trees surrounding them. After seeing Anne almost kissed by Lord Gillingham for a second time that day, Tobias had walked off, his thoughts in need of peace and quiet.

Still, Louisa's words continued to echo in his head.

Yes, she was right. He needed to speak to Anne. But how? What ought he to say? Tobias shook his head, for whenever he thought of addressing her, his mind went blank as though all words had tumbled out of his ears. It was a strange sickness indeed! Did all men suffer from it when they lost their hearts? Or was it only him?

In truth, Tobias could not imagine his brother ever at a loss.

"Anne is looking for you," Phineas elaborated, the look in his gaze watchful.

"I thought she'd gone inside with Lady Leonora."

Phineas shrugged. "Well, since she's free to come and go as she pleases..." His voice trailed off and his brows rose into arches as he looked at Tobias. "Can we focus on what's truly important here? Anne is looking for you and," he looked Tobias up and down, "she looks about as nervous as you do." The usual chuckle followed that observation.

Tobias tried to ignore the somersault his heart performed in that moment. "Where is she?"

"Near the maze," Phineas told him. "You should go and find her."

Indeed, he should. But what then?

"And you should hurry."

Tobias tensed. "Why?"

Grinning, his brother leaned a shoulder against a tall tree trunk. "Because I saw Lord Gillingham move toward her when I stepped away, and we all know what his intentions are, do we not?" His brows wiggled meaningfully.

Tobias wanted to slap that smug smile off his brother's face. Instead, however, he cursed under his breath and rushed past him. His feet moved with a swiftness he would not have thought possible, and his gaze darted past the lake the moment he stepped out of the grove. The tall-growing hedges on the other side of the large house were easy enough to spot, people rushing in and out, shrieking and laughing as snowballs flew in all directions.

Quickening his steps, Tobias crossed the snow-covered lawn before his eyes fell on Anne standing on a small slope near the maze with none other than Lord Gillingham. Tobias could have groaned as a physical pain shot through his middle and then reached up to squeeze his heart, holding it in a painful grip as another breath struggled past his lips.

While Lord Gillingham seemed to edge closer, Anne was all but leaning away from him. Her chin rose and she squared her shoulders in a way that made Tobias smile and sent a sense of pride through him. She was indeed beautiful and breathtaking, but also brave and bold and-

His heart faltered in his chest when Anne took a step back but was immediately pursued by Lord Gillingham. The man's face looked tense, and he appeared more than a bit reluctant to respect Anne's demand for more distance.

Gritting his teeth, Tobias suddenly felt a snowball whir past him.

His head flew around, his eyes sweeping over the many guests still playfully engaged in a wintry war before they returned to Anne.

Then he stilled, and a dark smile came to his face as he sank down and scooped snow into his hands, packing it tightly into a hard, unyielding ball.

By now, Tobias was no more than a few dozen feet away, and while he certainly could have called out or simply rushed over, in that moment he chose option three.

Pulling back his arm, he took aim and then sent the snowball flying.

Of course, years had passed since he'd last hurled such a missile; however, it seemed Fortune smiled on him that day. His aim was true, and the snowball hit Lord Gillingham square on the cheek, knocking him off his feet.

Anne looked momentarily taken aback. However, when her gaze found his, such a luminous smile spread over her face that Tobias wanted to kiss her then and there.

Instead, he rushed up to her, held out his hand and said, "Come with me."

Without a single glance at the man on the ground, Anne grasped his hand and then followed him into the maze, laughter spilling from their mouths as they hurried through the snow.

Away from Gillingham.

Away from Phineas.

Away from Lady Louisa.

Away.

## Chapter Fourteen

### MINE TO KISS

Anne thought her heart would pound out of her chest as she followed Tobias through the deep snow. The hem of her skirts was soaked and her feet felt chilled, but she didn't care. All she cared about was her hand in his, warm and safe.

With each step, the rest of the world fell away as the sounds of laughter and shrieking dimmed. The tall, snow-covered hedges hid them, wrapping them in a place of their own as though no one else existed but them.

Still, they moved onward until they reached the center of the maze, a stone bench flanked by two oak trees, standing like sentinels on each side. The snow on the ground looked untouched, their footprints the first to leave their marks. Stillness lingered as soft flakes began to drift downward from the heavens. Only a few: one here, one there, dancing in the chilled air.

And then Tobias stopped and turned to look at her, his hand still holding hers. She could see his warm breath like a puff of smoke as it mingled with the icy air around them, his cheeks flushed red. His eyes looked darker than they usually did, the clear, bright snow putting them into a stark contrast. Still, the same familiar warmth lingered in his gaze as he looked at her. "Is it true?" he asked then, and his hand tugged on hers, urging her a step closer.

Anne swallowed, noting the change in the way he was looking at her. "Is what true?"

He inhaled a deep breath, and the pad of his thumb brushed over her knuckles, sending another one of those teasing, tingling shivers down her back. "Do you love me?"

Anne's heart stilled in shock. "But, of course, I do," she laughed, afraid to be the first to say it out loud. "How can you not know that? I've loved you all my life."

Tobias's lips thinned, but the right corner of his mouth quirked slightly, telling her that he understood without a doubt what she was doing. That she was afraid. "I meant," he began, once again urging her a step closer, "are you *in love* with me?"

Anne could not help but wish the ground would open and swallow her whole. Instead, heat rushed to her cheeks as mortification burnt through her. *Please, do not let him laugh at me!*

A smile teased his lips. "Your cousin suggested that…"

*Curse Louisa!* "She simply meant that I care for you greatly as I always have."

Slowly, Tobias shook his head. "That is not what it sounded like. Indeed, she made it unmistakably clear that you-"

In a near panic, Anne withdrew her hand from his and took a few steps backward. "I do believe a more pressing question is why you attacked Lord Gillingham with such viciousness. The poor man was knocked off his feet!" Anne knew very well that she didn't care about Lord Gillingham. Nor was she concerned with Tobias's anger toward him. What Anne did know was that while Tobias had inquired after her feelings, he had yet to confess his own.

If indeed they existed!

Tobias's gaze narrowed and his eyes darkened. The warm chocolate-brown disappeared, replaced by a menacing black that made Anne wish she'd not said a word. Still, there was no turning back. At least, now, they were speaking about something other than her affections toward him. "You've always been such a kind and respectful man. Why were you so aggressive toward Lord Gillingham?"

His jaw tensed. "Because of you."

"Me?" Anne all but stammered, her gaze locked on his as he began to move toward her.

"You," Tobias confirmed, following her step by step as she retreated. "I loathe that man because whenever I see him, he's near you, asking you to dance or escorting you to supper or taking you for a stroll around the gardens." The words shot out of his mouth like bullets fired, their impact almost deafening. His gaze was sharp, harsh even, reminding her of a wolf stalking its prey. "Twice today, he tried to kiss you," he growled out, "and from the way he was looking at you just now, he-"

Anne shrank back for never in her life had she seen Tobias like this. He frightened her, but he also gave her hope. "What is it to you?" she demanded, daring him to answer. "Why would you care who kisses me?"

Tobias surged toward her, his hands gripping her upper arms as her back collided with one of the oak tree's unyielding trunk. "Because you're mine to kiss," he whispered against her lips, his eyes holding hers, open and honest, and yet, searching.

Anne drew in a shuddering breath. "Am I?" she asked as her heart began to dance in her chest. She felt a small tug on her lips and noted Tobias's hard gaze soften when he saw it.

"Yes, you are," he replied with a smile, the look in his eyes whispering of the same overwhelming emotions Anne felt course through her own veins. "You've always been."

"And yet," she pointed out, savoring the way he held her close, "you've never kissed me before today."

His gaze drifted to her lips before returning to meet her eyes. "I've been a fool," he whispered, and his left hand brushed along the line of her jaw and then slipped into her hair. "I, too, have loved you for as long as I can remember, but..." He sighed. "Something changed *that night* at the ball."

Without asking, Anne knew which ball he meant. "For me as well."

A relieved breath whispered past his lips. "Is it true then?" Tobias asked, deepest longing in his gaze. "Do you love me?"

Anne smiled, no longer afraid. "I've always loved you, but lately..."

"Lately?" His breath came fast as he looked down at her.

Feeling bold and daring, Anne pushed herself up onto her toes and pressed a kiss on Tobias's lips. It was no more than a soft pressure of mouth on mouth until he pulled her deeper into his embrace, his hand angling her head. He returned her kiss then, gentle and tentative, as they took the first steps away from the friendship that had connected them for as long as they could remember.

It was a daring leap, filled with uncertainty, but it also whispered of promises.

His lips teased hers apart as his hands slid under her cloak, touching her in a way a friend never would. She felt his caresses through the thick fabric of her woolen gown as his hands brushed up her back, then down and to the front, running over her ribcage before settling on her waist. He held her close, their warmth mingling, as he deepened the kiss, taking it far beyond what they had shared earlier that morning in the library.

It felt as though a lifetime had passed since then.

Eager for more, Anne trailed her hands upward, sliding her palms over his broad chest and up to his shoulders. Her fingertips danced along the side of his neck, feeling warm skin as well as a pulse that beat as fast as her own. Her hands slipped into his hair as she pulled herself closer. In answer, his arms wrapped around her, holding her tightly, promising to never let her go again.

When they finally pulled apart, they were both out of breath, but the joy they saw on each other's faces was palpable. Never had Anne seen Tobias's eyes as bright nor his smile as radiant as they were in that moment.

And it was for her.

*Because of* her.

As hers was because of him.

"Promise me," Tobias began, a smile on his face, but his voice heavy with emotion, "that you'll never let that man anywhere near you ever again." He said it lightly, and yet, Anne understood the depth of his fears.

The thought that she could be lost to him.

Brushing a hand over his cheek, she smiled up at the man she loved, the man who'd been her friend all her life. "I never cared for him. Surely, you must know that." She felt his chest rise and then fall as a deep breath rushed from his lungs. "Besides, I can think of a fairly simple way to ensure that he'll never come near me again." Her brows rose teasingly, and Tobias laughed.

"Would you consent to marry me then, *Friend*?" he teased as he lowered his head, leaning his forehead against hers. "So, I may call you *Wife? Darling? Beloved*?"

Anne could have sighed hearing these endearments from his lips. "I must say you make marriage sound so very tempting." Her eyes held his for she needed him to hear her, to truly hear her. "But the reason I agree is simply because I happen to be in love with you."

His heart skipped a beat-she could feel it against the palm of her hand-before his lips claimed hers in a quick, but lingering kiss. "I love you as well," Tobias whispered, his breath uneven. "I love you like a man loves a woman, and I want you now and forever."

"Now and forever," Anne echoed before she sank into Tobias's arms once more. The world around them disappeared as thousands of snowflakes began to dance around the tall, unyielding oak as though in celebration of their love.

Attending Lord Archibald's house party had been a wise choice indeed.

# Epilogue

*Barrington House, England, Spring 1802 (or a variation thereof)*

Anne's hand felt warm and soft within his own as Tobias tugged her through the door and then pushed it closed with a kick of his boot.

"We will be miss-" she objected before he pulled her into his arms, sealing her lips with a deep kiss. His hands slid over her gown, feeling her tempting curves beneath, wishing the day had already come and gone. "You're making it very hard for me to keep my wits about me," she sighed when he trailed kisses down her throat.

Tobias chuckled, nipping gently at her skin, "I've waited long enough for this day."

"As have I," Anne replied as she pushed him back, her deep blue eyes finding his. "But this is our wedding day. What will our families think when we simply disappear from our wedding breakfast?"

A wicked grin came to his face.

Laughing, Anne slapped his shoulder. "I never knew you possessed such roguish tendencies, Mr. Hawke," she chided him. "I must say I'm discovering all new sides to you now that I'm your wife."

"Are you disappointed?"

A slow smile spread over her lovely face. "I didn't say that, now did I?"

Impatience burnt in Tobias's veins as he pulled her into another deep kiss, overwhelmed by how life had changed in the past few months. While Anne was still his friend and they continued to tease and laugh as they always had, she was now so much more than that as well. There was a deeper understanding, a bond that went beyond what they'd previously shared. Every day, they discovered something new about one another and, every night, he fell asleep with a deliriously happy smile upon his lips.

"Ah! There you are!"

Cursing Anne's meddlesome cousin, Tobias reluctantly released his vice-like hold upon his wife and took a step back. He hadn't even heard Louisa approach, let alone enter the room; however, judging from the disapproving look on Anne's face, his wife had been equally oblivious.

"What are you doing here?" Anne asked her cousin, her hands quickly moving to right the wrinkles Tobias's hands had left upon her gown.

"Looking for you," Louisa replied with a self-evident look in her eyes. "After all, it is your wedding day, and you cannot simply disappear without it being noted."

Anne cast him a meaningful look.

"Very well," Tobias relented, offering his wife his arm. "We'll return to share in the festivities."

"I think that is advisable," Louisa remarked as she stepped closer and tucked a loose strand behind Anne's left ear, a knowing grin upon her face. "I do love to see you two so happy," she told them then, her blue eyes moving from Anne to him before returning to his wife. "You must admit you're quite fortunate to have me as your family. After all, without my assistance, I doubt we'd be here today celebrating your union." Her brows rose meaningfully.

Tobias laughed, "Are you fishing for a compliment, *dear cousin*?"

Louisa smiled at him. "A thank-you will do, *dearest Tobias*."

Sighing, Tobias offered her a formal bow. "I'm offering you my deepest gratitude for your wisdom in urging us to recognize the bond between us." He smiled at Anne as she squeezed his arm, her eyes warm and glowing. "Your determination and selfless sacrifice shall never be forgotten."

Rolling her eyes at him, Louisa sighed, "I must say that is a very unbecoming quality," she miffed, her nose slightly wrinkled. "You sound just like your awful brother."

"That reminds me," Anne said as a slow, somewhat wicked smile came to her lips. "You have yet to fulfill your end of our bargain."

For a second, Tobias frowned before he remembered what Anne had told him about everything Louisa had done during their visit to Windmere Park to make the two of them see what was truly between them. Not only had she tackled Anne to the ground and given Tobias a good talking-to, but she'd also promised to kiss Phineas if Anne and Tobias ever were to tie the knot.

Now, they had.

"Will you forfeit?" Anne dared her.

Louisa's gaze hardened, and her jaw set in determination. "Never."

As though on cue, footsteps echoed to their ears from down the hall, and a moment later, Phineas poked his head into the room. "What are you all doing in here?" he asked, looking from one to the other.

Louisa groaned and turned back to glare at Anne. "You did this on purpose!" she hissed.

Anne merely shrugged, an innocent smile upon her face.

Tobias tried his utmost not to laugh.

Huffing out an annoyed breath, Louisa spun on her heel and marched up to a rather bewildered-looking Phineas. "Don't read anything into this," she told him before her hands seized his face and pulled him into a kiss.

Tobias couldn't help but stare at them, and neither could Anne, her hand now like an iron vice upon his arm.

Phineas seemed momentarily caught off guard as Louisa's lips claimed his; however, he quickly recovered, returning her kiss with utter enthusiasm. His hands settled on her waist, holding her to him when she made to pull away.

"I told you not to read anything into this," she snapped at Phineas, shoving him away with another annoyed eye roll. Then she turned to Anne, one brow arching upward. "There. Satisfied?"

Anne opened her mouth to reply; however, Phineas was faster. Tobias watched with wide eyes as his brother pulled Louisa back into his arms. "Far from it," he answered her question, a wide grin on his face. Then he dipped his head and kissed her again, cutting off her startled gasp.

Anne turned to her husband then, clutching his arm. "Your brother and my cousin?" she whispered, her eyes wide and her lips twitching as she grinned up at him.

Tobias chuckled, "I thought you suspected them from the start."

"I was merely jesting," Anne mumbled as her eyes darted back to the other two in the room. "But now..."

"Do you think they'd ever admit that they care for each other?" Tobias asked, surprised by his brother's strong reaction to Louisa. Was it possible that Phineas genuinely cared for her?

Anne shook her head. "Not in a thousand years. They're far too stubborn. Both of them."

Again, Louisa tried to free herself from Phineas's hold on her, her hands curling into his lapels and giving him a slight, rather feeble-looking push.

Tobias frowned. "Should we...interfere?" He glanced at Anne. "Should we...save her?"

Anne shook her head, grinning. "Oh, she's more than capable of saving herself. If she doesn't, perhaps she simply does not wish to be saved."

Smiling, Tobias pulled his wife into his arms. "This was to be our day," he whispered before he placed a gentle kiss upon her lips.

"It still is," Anne pointed out, a deeply seductive smile curling up the corners of her mouth. "Perhaps we should find another room." She glanced at Phineas and Louisa, who seemed to have forgotten the world around them. "One with fewer people in it."

Wrapping an arm around his wife's waist, Tobias pulled her from the room and out into the hall. "That is an excellent idea, *Wife*."

"Thank you, *Husband*," Anne laughed as they sneaked down the hallway, leaving the other two to figure this out on their own.

After all, what could happen?

THE END

Thank you for reading *Once Upon a Kiss Gone Horribly Wrong!*

Are you eager to find out what will happen between Louisa and Phineas?

They get their own story in *Once Upon a Devilishly Enchanting Kiss,* book 1 of the **Whickertons in Love** series.

# Also by Bree Wolf

THE WHICKERTONS IN LOVE

LOVE'S SECOND CHANCE SERIES: TALES OF LORDS & LADIES

LOVE'S SECOND CHANCE SERIES: TALES OF DAMSELS & KNIGHTS

ALSO BY BREE WOLF

LOVE'S SECOND CHANCE SERIES: HIGHLAND TALES

HAPPY EVER REGENCY SERIES

FORBIDDEN LOVE SERIES

For more information visit www.breewolf.com

# About Bree

USA Today bestselling and award-winning author, Bree Wolf has always been a language enthusiast (though not a grammarian!) and is rarely found without a book in her hand or her fingers glued to a keyboard. Trying to find her way, she has taught English as a second language, traveled abroad and worked at a translation agency as well as a law firm in Ireland. She also spent loooong years obtaining a BA in English and Education and an MA in Specialized Translation while wishing she could simply be a writer. Although there is nothing simple about being a writer, her dreams have finally come true.

"A big thanks to my fairy godmother!"

Currently, Bree has found her new home in the historical romance genre, writing Regency novels and novellas. Enjoying the mix of fact and fiction, she occasionally feels like a puppet master (or mistress? Although that sounds weird!), forcing her characters into ever-new situations that will put their strength, their beliefs, their love to the test, hoping that in the end they will triumph and get the happily-ever-after we are all looking for.

If you're an avid reader, sign up for Bree's newsletter on www.breewolf.com as she has the tendency to simply give books away. Find out about freebies, giveaways as well as occasional advance reader copies and read before the book is even on the shelves!

Connect with Bree and stay up-to-date on new releases:

facebook.com/breewolf.novels
twitter.com/breewolf_author
instagram.com/breewolf_author
amazon.com/Bree-Wolf/e/B00FJX27Z4
bookbub.com/authors/bree-wolf

Printed in Great Britain
by Amazon

23885967R00061